Mr Finney and the World Turned Upside-down

Amsterdam . Antwerpen
Em. Querido's Uitgeverij BV
2009

www.mrfinney.nl
www.queridokind.nl

Copyright text
© 2009 Laurentien van Oranje
Copyright illustrations
© 2009 Sieb Posthuma
Story line and characters
© 2009 Laurentien van Oranje en Sieb Posthuma
Copyright translation
© 2009 David Colmer

Design and layout
Bockting Ontwerpers, Amsterdam

ISBN 978 90 451 1064 6
NUR 281

Uitgeverij Querido does its utmost to use natural
resources in an environmentally friendly and
sustainable way. This book is made of paper that
meets the requirements of the Forest Stewardship
Council (FSC) label and is also totally chlorine free
(TCF). Its production did not contribute to forest
destruction.

Laurentien van Oranje &
Sieb Posthuma

Mr Finney

and the World Turned Upside-down

Translated by David Colmer

Home

The Journey

The Task

Home

The Looking Day

FIRST one eye opened, then the other. Mr Finney was waking from a deep sleep. He wiggled his toes, gave three big yawns and stretched his fins. Then, wide-awake, he looked up through the window above his head.

If the sky was blue, he would usually jump out of bed and go outside straightaway. But if it was cloudy, he would often stay there under the blankets for a moment to look up and count the clouds. If he picked out one cloud and stared at it, it might start to look like something. A house, a tree or an animal.

But not today. *Plonk, plonk, plonk...* Big fat raindrops fell from the sky and splashed loudly on the window.

How can I count clouds with this racket going on? thought Mr Finney. He got up, dressed and pulled on his favourite boots. They were the only boots he had and he liked them very much.

Mr Finney would have preferred to stay in bed. He stomped into the kitchen and looked out through the window. The view didn't make him feel any better: rain, rain and more rain! But the longer Mr Finney looked, the more excited he grew. The rain made everything outside look different. The tree trunks were gleaming as smooth as worms.

The flowers struggled to keep their heads above water. Little streams he'd never seen before were flowing through his garden. The rainwater barrel was almost overflowing.

'I'm not sure I've ever seen rain this heavy,' Mr Finney whispered to himself. He wondered if it had been raining all night, and thought about what to do. Maybe a cup of tea and a biscuit to start the day?

After a sip and a nibble in the big chair by the window, he felt better. Being dry in the house with all that rain outside was actually quite cosy. He was just settling down with this thought in mind when there was a knock on the door.

'Who is it?' asked Mr Finney. He never had visitors this early in the morning.

'It's me, Snail.'

Mr Finney always had time for Snail, because Snail was his friend. He usually had a good story to tell, even if it took Mr Finney a while to work out what the story was about. That was because Snail was so slow: by the time he reached the end of a story, Mr Finney had almost forgotten how it started. But Snail was like that.

Mr Finney opened the door, almost bumping his nose on Snail, who looked like he'd just got out of the bath and forgotten to dry himself. Snail gave Mr Finney a sad look. Even the two feelers on his head were drooping, instead of sticking up cheerfully like usual. It didn't look like Snail had come to tell him a funny story this time.

'Snail, what's the matter?' asked Mr Finney.

'Can I come in out of the rain?' asked Snail.

'Of course,' Mr Finney replied, 'but why do you need to? You always have your own house with you.'

'Yes,' said Snail, 'but when you carry your roof on your head, the sound of the rain can drive you crazy.'

Mr Finney didn't like the tapping above his head, so he could understand Snail hating the tapping on his head even more. He hurried into the kitchen to get a cup of tea and a biscuit for Snail.

Snail sighed as he sat down. 'My tea always goes cold, Mr Finney. I'm just too slow. But I like cold tea too!'

'You're so funny,' Mr Finney answered. 'I'm glad you've come. Because you know what, Snail? Today I'm having a looking day. Nice and cosy, from the chair by the window.'

'A looking day?' asked Snail. 'What are you looking at?'

'All kinds of things. Things inside the house and things outside. I see things inside my head too. And then I look at all the things I see and think about. It's like going on a trip.' Mr Finney was quite pleased that he had done such a good job of explaining what a looking day was.

'Oh, you mean travelling inside your head,' said Snail. 'I do that too, because I'm too slow to really travel. In my head I can go as fast as I like.'

Mr Finney and Snail sat there for a while, looking out, until the first rain stopped and the second rain started. The second rain was what Mr Finney called the raindrops that slid off the leaves after the rain had stopped falling from the sky.

'After it rains, it drips,' Mr Finney said.

'Imagine if it kept raining forever,' said Snail, 'then we'd float away or drown.'

'First my barrel would overflow and then my whole garden,' Mr Finney said. 'And then anyone who can't swim or doesn't have fins like mine would be in trouble.' Now he thought about it, Mr Finney was very glad he had feet *and* fins. That way he could walk or swim, whichever he needed.

'If that happens,' said Snail, 'I'll turn my shell into a boat and sail downstream.' It sounded like something he'd been planning for a while. 'Is that a good idea?' he asked.

'Definitely,' Mr Finney agreed. 'But look, the rain really has stopped now. Let's go outside!' He jumped up and ran through the kitchen into the garden.

'It smells so lovely!' he called happily while spinning around in circles. He held his fins out and breathed deeply. 'I smell rain and drops of water and grass and flowers! Look over there at the birds in that tree! Look, Snail, look around!'

'I'm coming, I'm coming!' Snail cried from the doorway. Mr Finney was already at the bottom of the garden, sitting on the lowest branch of the biggest tree. Since the day he first saw it, it had been Mr Finney's favourite tree. Happy and contented, he looked out over his garden. He had arranged everything and given it all a place: the shrubs and flowers and the vegetables in his vegetable garden. The only thing he hadn't decided was the location of his favourite tree, which had been there its whole life.

He looked from the fence to his house and back again, and he looked out at the line beyond the fence, at the end of the fields around his house. 'That's the horizon,' Owl had once told him. Owl was his neighbour. 'The world beyond the horizon is much bigger than your garden. The world is a big globe and there's a horizon everywhere.' Mr Finney remembered exactly how Owl had peered at him through his round glasses. He didn't see him often, because Owl was awake at night when Mr Finney was asleep. And when Mr Finney was awake, Owl was asleep.

When Snail finally reached the tree, he asked Mr Finney, 'What are you looking at and what do you see?'

It took a while for Mr Finney to answer. 'What am I looking at and what do I see?' he repeated softly. 'That's a good question, Snail. Because looking and seeing aren't the same thing. Sometimes you don't really see something even though it's there. Like sunlight shining through trees. Or dewdrops on a spider web. Or the twilight, just before it gets dark. They're all things we miss if we don't look closely!'

'Shall we look together?' asked Snail, who was finally sitting on Mr Finney's branch. 'Then we'll see twice as much!'

The two friends looked out silently. Mr Finney wiggled his toes and Snail's feelers were sticking up again. The trunks of the trees were almost dry. Suddenly they felt the branches and leaves shaking. They looked at each other with big eyes. *Frrrrrrr*, went the leaves and branches of Mr Finney's favourite tree. *Frrrrrrrrrrrrrr*!

'Mr Finney, did you feel that too?' asked Snail.

'Yes, I felt it too,' whispered Mr Finney. 'It was the wind, wasn't it?'

Snail swallowed. 'If it was, wouldn't the other trees be shaking too, Mr Finney?' he asked quietly. He was trembling. 'It's as if something is flying around us without our being able to see it.'

'That's exactly what I was getting at, Snail. Sometimes you don't see something even when it's there.' Mr Finney tried hard not to look frightened and hoped that Snail would stop trembling too. 'Don't be scared,' he added, even though he was just as confused about why the tree was shaking.

Mr Finney and Snail looked out over the fields silently for a moment. The sun broke through and they felt its warmth on their backs. They were glad it had stopped raining.

'Look!' Mr Finney shouted suddenly, pointing into the distance with a fin. An enormous rainbow had appeared out of nowhere on the horizon.

MR FINNEY and Snail stayed in the tree for a while. They couldn't get enough of looking at the rainbow on the horizon.

'Do you think we're the only ones who can see the rainbow?' asked Snail after a long silence.

'That's a good question,' Mr Finney replied. 'When I look at the night sky from in my bed, I often ask myself, 'Can everyone see the moon and the stars or am I the only one?' And then I wonder how big the sky is. But no matter how hard I rack my brains, I can't work it out. Because the sky is so big, it doesn't fit into my head.'

Snail was quiet for a moment. Then he said, 'Maybe there are animals living on the other side of the rainbow, and they're looking at it just like we are.'

Mr Finney nodded. 'Which colour of the rainbow do you think is the most beautiful?' he asked after a while.

Snail thought about it.

'The most beautiful colour isn't there!'

'Huh?' Mr Finney glanced sideways at Snail. 'Your voice sounds funny!'

'I didn't say anything,' Snail said. 'I'm still thinking! That voice came from under us!'

'Really?' asked Mr Finney.

Snail nodded so hard his feelers wobbled.

'It's got all the colours: red, orange, yellow, green, blue and violet. But they forgot the most beautiful one!' the voice said indignantly.

Mr Finney and Snail didn't know where to look. First the voice had come from the bottom of the tree, now it came from the branch above them. When they looked up they saw two dangling legs. Each foot was in a glittering pink shoe with a bow on it. Now and then the heels clicked together.

'Don't you think it's strange they forgot pink?'

Now they saw whose voice it was. It was the prettiest creature they had ever seen. She was half girl and half something else. On her back she wore two pink wings that were so thin you could see right through them.

'Who are you?' Mr Finney asked shyly. 'And where do you come from?'

With a beaming smile the creature answered, 'I'm Pinky Pepper. I'm from everywhere and nowhere. And you?'

She was so beautiful and she looked so sweet! Mr Finney couldn't keep his eyes off her and Snail was at a loss for words.

'I, er... I'm Snail, and this, um... this is Mr Finney,' said Snail.

'Snail is my friend!' Mr Finney added.

'Do you live here?' asked Pinky Pepper. 'Or have you just glimped in?'

'We live here. Snail lives in the house on his back and I live in my own house,' Mr Finney said, pointing to the other end of the garden. 'What's glimping?'

'Don't you know what glimping is?' Pinky Pepper asked with surprise. 'Shall I show you?'

Strange
Discoveries

And before Mr Finney and Snail could blink their eyes, she disappeared in a pink flash. *Frrrrrrrrrrrrrrr*. And then they heard from the top of the tree, 'Yoo-hoo! Can you see me?' *Frrrrrrrrrrrrrrrr*. 'And now?'

'That was really fast!' Mr Finney said excitedly.

'You can say that again,' said Snail. 'I've never seen anything that fast before!'

They saw another glittering flash and now Pinky Pepper was sitting on Mr Finney's chimney. Snail and Mr Finney almost fell off the branch with astonishment.

'How do you do that?' Mr Finney called out to her.

Just when Snail was about to ask if it was scary up on top of the house, Pinky Pepper reappeared next to them on the branch.

'So,' she said, smoothing her pink skirt. 'That's glimping. Did you like it? I just went from the tree to the chimney, but I can go a lot higher and a lot further. I go around the whole world like that!'

'Isn't it dangerous?' asked Snail.

'Not at all,' Pinky Pepper laughed. 'But I never stay anywhere long, no matter how much fun it is. There's too much to see in the world! Do you two ever travel? Maybe we could go together sometime.'

'I only travel in my head,' Snail said. 'I'm much too slow for a real trip.'

Mr Finney nodded. 'I always travel in my head too, and sometimes through my garden and through my house. It never gets boring because I always see something else.'

'Mr Finney built his whole house himself,' Snail said proudly. 'Mr Finney can make anything that pops into his head.'

Mr Finney didn't like other people talking about him, so he started whistling. That gave him a chance to think about all the things he'd like to ask.

But Pinky Pepper beat him to it. 'Can you sit a bit closer together?' she asked.

Surprised, Mr Finney and Snail exchanged glances and slid a little closer. Pinky Pepper pulled a small device out of her pink handbag and pointed it at Mr Finney and Snail. 'Smile!' she said while pushing a button.

'What's that?' asked Snail. 'Can I see?'

'Of course,' Pinky Pepper giggled, 'This is my SuperBeeBee!'

'Your super-what?' Mr Finney asked.

'My SuperBeeBee. It's a phone, camera and video camera in one. I use it to write letters and read about all kinds of things, and it shows me exactly where I am. So I know which way to glimp!'

'This is all too fast for me!' Snail said, shaking his head. He slid off the branch slowly and disappeared under a shrub.

Pinky Pepper fluttered her eyelashes.

'Shall I show you how it works?' she asked. She sat next to Mr Finney and patiently demonstrated everything: there was a button to turn her SuperBeeBee on and off, and other buttons with numbers and letters on them. She explained that each picture on the screen did something else. Mr Finney's eyes grew bigger.

'If you touch the picture of the telephone, you can call someone. And if you touch the picture of the letter, you can send someone a letter.'

'Who?' Mr Finney asked inquisitively.

'Well, anyone you know who has a SuperBee-Bee,' Pinky Pepper replied.

Mr Finney was glad she explained it so well.

Then Pinky Pepper tapped the picture of the camera. 'And these are photos I've taken while glimping. Look: this is a photo of a forest, taken from high up in the air. And this is a desert and these are snow-capped mountains.' Pinky Pepper kept pressing a button to move on to the next photo. 'And this is an ocean. Have you ever seen this much water?'

Mr Finney thought of the water in his garden when it was raining. Pinky Pepper pressed the button again. Now Mr Finney saw a photo of towers with grey smoke pouring out of them.

'What's that?' Mr Finney asked, swinging his legs. It was hard to sit still while he was seeing so many exciting things.

'They're called factories. They're big buildings where they make all kinds of things,' Pinky
Pepper pressed the button again. 'And this is a
city, with busy streets where everyone's crowded
together. And this is a flag on the seabed.'

Mr Finney didn't quite get it. 'What's a flag
doing…'

But Pinky Pepper jumped up. 'It's time to
glimp on. There's so much more to discover in
the world.' She brushed his cheek with her left
wing. 'See you soon!'

Frrrrrrrrrrr, felt Mr Finney. It no longer
frightened him now that he knew what it was,
but he was still surprised by how fast she disappeared.

'Next time I come, I'll tell you what else I've
seen!' Pinky Pepper shouted down from above
the trees.

'When will that be?' Mr Finney called back,
looking up. But all he saw was a glittering pink
flash.

In the Middle of the
Night

PINKY PEPPER had disappeared as suddenly as she had come. And Snail too was nowhere to be seen. Mr Finney climbed down from his favourite tree and went into the house. He wanted nothing more than to go straight to bed. His head was full of all that had happened. Where had Pinky Pepper glimped off to now?

Mr Finney wondered how that glimping of hers worked. 'Maybe glimping isn't much more than looking around you,' he said to himself. 'I do that too. Just not as high and not as far.'

He opened the window above his bed and jumped in under the covers. Just a bit of reading, then lights off. After which Mr Finney would usually fall straight to sleep. He grabbed a book from the pile next to his bed and opened it up to where he had stopped reading the day before. But the letters danced in front of his eyes and he kept starting over again at the top of the page. So many things were running through his mind at the same time that he couldn't follow the story. He put down the book, turned off the light, closed his eyes and tried to sleep.

But Mr Finney just tossed and turned. He thought of Pinky Pepper and her dancing eyelashes. For a moment he almost felt her wing brush his cheek again. He felt a tingling when he thought of her. And it tingled even more when he thought about glimping: what would it be like to see the world outside his fence with his own two eyes?

Mr Finney sat up and turned on his bedside lamp. He knew that he should turn off the light if he wanted to sleep, but tonight everything was different. His own thoughts were driving him crazy. If only he had someone to talk to! But who? Everyone was asleep!

Mr Finney got up and carefully made his way to the kitchen. In the daytime he knew just where everything was, but he had never walked through his house in the dark before. 'Ouch!' cried Mr Finney, bumping his toe on a cupboard. He ran his fins along the wall until he found the light switch, then turned on the light.

He drank a glass of water and was about to go back to bed when he heard someone tapping on the kitchen window. He looked out and straight into the eyes of his neighbour, Owl. He opened the door. 'Hello, Owl, what a surprise! Were you passing by?'

'Not really,' answered Owl. 'I was in the forest when I saw the light on in your house. That was so unusual I was worried there might be some kind of problem.'

'I'm so glad to see you!' Mr Finney said. 'It's nothing really, but, well... there is something. My head is so full of questions and thoughts that I can't sleep. I was lying in bed thinking and tossing and turning, so I got up to drink some water.'

'And what were you thinking? What was keeping you awake?' Owl asked.

Mr Finney told him about all the things that had happened. About meeting Pinky Pepper, glimping and her photos of the world.

Owl was quiet for a moment. 'I understand most of those things, Mr Finney,' he said. 'I might not be able to glimp, but I've still seen a lot of the world. I often fly over rivers, fields and forests. And sometimes, very rarely, I come to the outskirts of cities, where things look totally different.'

'You mean one of those busy places with crowded streets?' Mr Finney asked, remembering the photo on the SuperBeeBee.

'That's right, with lots of tall buildings,' Owl said.

'And have you ever seen a flag on the bottom of the sea?' Mr Finney asked cautiously. He was curious what Owl would say now.

'I've never seen anything like that!' Owl replied, without a moment's hesitation. 'I have seen a lot of seas, though, and they're definitely worth it.'

'Worth what?' asked Mr Finney.

'Worth travelling. Why don't you go travelling yourself? So you can see the world?'

'Travelling? Me?' Mr Finney exclaimed. 'I've never been outside my garden!'

Owl looked at Mr Finney and saw that he really was a little confused. 'Get some sleep first. Think about travelling tomorrow when you're not so tired. It's not scary. It's actually a lot of fun!' He gave Mr Finney a nod, flew out through the kitchen door and disappeared into the dark night.

Suddenly Mr Finney realised how tired he was. He turned off the kitchen light and walked to his bedroom. For the second time that night Mr Finney climbed into bed. He could hardly wait to tell Snail about his conversation with Owl.

Everything   Goes

Wrong

M R FINNEY jumped out of bed as soon as he saw the blue sky. No rain today!

Strange that I still feel so tired, he thought. *I'll have a bath first, that should help.*

He turned on the tap and poured some bubble bath into his glass bathtub. Sitting in the hot water, he felt awake at last. Splash, splash, splash! Playfully, he smacked the froth with his fins. But then he remembered why he was so tired: he'd gone to sleep late because he'd had so much to think about. 'Hardly surprising,' he mumbled to himself, 'since meeting Pinky Pepper I've been thinking non-stop!'

As the water cooled off, Mr Finney grew restless. He climbed out of the bath, dried himself and got dressed. But when he took a step his feet felt funny! There was something wrong with them. Mr Finney looked down. At first he couldn't see anything out of the ordinary, but then he realised. He'd put his boots on the wrong way round! The right boot was on his left foot and his left boot was on his right foot. Mr Finney burst out laughing. How could he be so silly? He kicked off his boots and changed them round. *That's more comfortable*, he thought, walking out the door.

Mr Finney sat down on the rocking chair on his veranda. When he wasn't sitting on the lowest branch of his favourite tree, he liked to sit on this old chair.

He whistled a tune to the rhythm of his rocking. But suddenly he heard a strange sound. *Squeeeak! Squeeeeak!* Was a bird he'd never heard before sitting in the tree? *Sqeeeeak!* he heard again. Or was it a mouse? The sound was very close by. *Squeeak!* When Mr Finney stopped rocking, so did the sound. 'Strange,' said Mr Finney, 'the noise is coming from under my rocking chair!' He stood up, bent forward and saw that one of the legs was loose.

Mr Finney never got upset when things broke or wore out because he loved fixing them. He went to the shed to fetch his toolbox and a box of nails. When he had everything he needed, he turned the chair upside down. He held a nail in place with his fin and gave it a hard bang with the hammer. 'Ouch!' Instead of hitting the nail, Mr Finney had hit his own fin. He sighed and tried again. Again he hit his own fin. 'Ouch!'

What was the matter with him today? Everything was going wrong! First his boots, then the loose leg of the chair, and now this! *Third time lucky*, thought Mr Finney, who was getting angry with himself. Surely he was able to hammer a nail into a loose leg of a chair? He grabbed the hammer again, held the nail in place and swung at it. 'Ouch!' He couldn't believe he'd mishit three times in a row. *I think I'd better go sit on my branch*, thought Mr Finney. *At least nothing can go wrong there.*

Walking to his favourite tree, he discovered a big pile of beechnut shells in the middle of the path. *Left there by the squirrel of course*, thought Mr Finney angrily. The squirrel and his friends gobbled up the nuts one after the other and threw the shells into Mr Finney's garden. Then Mr Finney had to rake his garden again to avoid tripping over the mess. The squirrel couldn't care less. Grumbling, Mr Finney carried on to his favourite tree.

Snail had been woken up by the sound of hammering and had started his morning walk. A little later he reached the tree Mr Finney was sitting in and called up, 'Good morning, Mr Finney!'

Mr Finney didn't seem to hear him.

Snail called out again, 'Good morning!'

Mr Finney still stared into space.

'GOOD MOR-NING!' Snail screamed up into the tree.

Mr Finney jumped. 'What, um... who's there?' he stammered. He bent forward and looked down. 'Oh. It's you, Snail...' And while saying this, he wobbled and fell off his branch – Boom! – landing in the grass next to Snail with a loud smack.

'What's wrong?' Snail asked. 'Didn't you hear me? And why did you fall out of the tree? You've never done that before. What's got into you?'

'Don't ask, Snail,' Mr Finney replied. 'I couldn't sleep last night because I kept thinking about Pinky Pepper. She's so pretty and it's such a strange feeling to have her whizzing around. And I thought what a shame it is that she never wants to stay in one spot.'

Snail smiled as Mr Finney continued. 'And I thought about all the photos she showed me on the screen of her SuperBeebee. Oh, Snail, if you'd seen those photos, you'd know exactly how I feel!'

'You're just a bit in love,' said Snail.

Mr Finney turned to look at Snail. 'In love? Me? Not true!' he cried. 'Really, I'm not!'

Snail laughed, because he'd only said it to tease Mr Finney.

Mr Finney continued. 'There are so many things I want to ask her about the world. Do you think she'll come back?'

'Probably,' Snail said. 'Didn't she say something about 'next time' when she was leaving?'

'You're right, Snail. She did say that,' agreed Mr Finney, who could hardly stand still.

'So what's the problem?' Snail asked, giving Mr Finney a sideways glance.

'I don't know. After yesterday everything here seems so different. So small. The things Pinky Pepper showed me were so much bigger. And so exciting!'

'I'm not fast and I'm not exciting,' Snail said, 'but we can still travel in our heads and around the garden, can't we? You haven't forgotten that, have you?'

'No, of course I haven't forgotten, Snail,'
Mr Finney said. He rubbed his bottom with his
fin, because he really had come down with a
bump. 'But try to understand. Look at my tree.
I always thought it was the biggest tree in the
whole world! But now I've seen forests full of
trees that look much bigger than mine!'

'But you've seen those forests now, haven't
you?' said Snail. 'On the SuperBeeBee. What
more do you want?'

'I want to see it all with my own eyes,' Mr
Finney replied. 'The forests, the desert, the
mountains and the hills. I want to see busy
streets and buildings that touch the clouds.'

Snail was starting to get worried. 'Mr Finney,'
he said, 'that's all too far away for animals like
us. We're too small to walk that far. We don't
have wings to fly like Owl and the other birds.
And we can't glimp like Pinky Pepper.' He
looked to see whether Mr Finney was listening,
but he was just staring straight ahead. 'That's
why we stay here and travel inside our heads!'
Snail added in an emphatic voice. He hoped that
would put an end to Mr Finney's worrying.

Mr Finney was still staring ahead without
saying anything. 'Maybe you're right,' he said
after a while.

Snail smiled.

'But still...' Suddenly Mr Finney thought of his
conversation with Owl. 'Even Owl said I should
go travelling if I wanted to see everything for
myself! And he said it wasn't scary either.'

Snail had no answer to that.

Now Mr Finney really was confused. He had come out and said what was on his mind, but he had no idea how to go travelling. Snail was right about that. 'I'll just see to what needs doing here in the garden first,' he mumbled. 'The rest will come later.' He walked back to his shed to get the wheelbarrow.

Snail slid along behind him as fast as he could. 'Shall I help you with the weeding and the beechnut shells?' he asked.

'Yes, please,' Mr Finney said. 'There's a lot to do!'

And so Snail and Mr Finney walked together from one side of the garden to the other. They picked up every shell they saw and pulled up all the weeds, roots and all. They hardly said anything to each other all day, but it was still a lot of fun. *That's because we're friends*, thought Snail happily. *Friends understand each other without words*.

When they were finished at the end of the day, they flopped down next to each other on the lawn. 'It helps, doesn't it?' said Snail contentedly. 'A day working in the garden together always clears your mind.'

Mr Finney nodded. But he had actually spent the whole day thinking about Pinky Pepper and the world outside his garden. His mind was made up: he would go travelling to see the world with his own eyes. He just had to work out how.

The

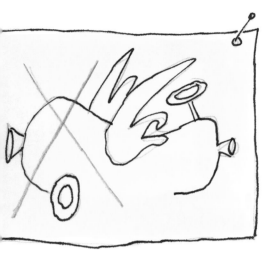

MR FINNEY was tired from all that gardening. He felt like going straight to bed but decided to clean up the shed first. He couldn't stop thinking about his conversation with Snail and he kept hearing himself say that he wanted to go travelling. But Snail was right: Mr Finney had no idea how. He loved walking, but that would hardly be enough for this trip. Hadn't Owl said something about flying a very long way? He needed to come up with something that could carry him further than his own two legs.

Mr Finney liked being in his shed. If he had something to do and wanted to be alone for a while, this was his favourite spot. It was a place for thinking about things, but always things he wanted to make or fix. He always started off with a drawing. Then he'd build a small version of what he'd drawn. If there was the slightest thing wrong with it, he'd start all over again. Mr Finney didn't start building for real until the design was perfect. The biggest thing he had made up till now was his house. He had spent night after night drawing, followed by weeks of building.

Mr Finney walked around his shed. He stopped at a wall on which five different hammers were hung up neatly in place.

Invention

With his fin he traced the black lines he had drawn around them so that he would always know which hammer to hang where. Then he looked into the box where he stored the screwdrivers, punches and saws. Next to them were the trays with nails and screws, all sorted according to type and size: big ones with big ones and little ones with little ones.

Mr Finney pulled open a drawer and took out a sheet of paper. He put his pencil on the blank sheet and sighed. He didn't really know what he wanted to make. He started pacing back and forth in the shed. His thoughts kept returning to Pinky Pepper. He smiled. Wasn't she sweet! He saw her before him with her shining eyes. There was nothing he would like more than to glimp somewhere together with her...

'Wait a minute!' Mr Finney exclaimed. 'To glimp you need wings, of course!' He ran back to his piece of paper and started drawing wings. Narrow wings and round wings, big wings and small wings, thick wings and thin wings. He drew and drew until his piece of paper was covered with wings. He took another sheet and kept on drawing until it started to get dark. Then he stood up to turn on the light.

Mr Finney looked at the wings he had drawn. *But I'm not a bird and I'm not Pinky Pepper either*, he thought. He sat down on the edge of his wheelbarrow. 'If I'm not a bird,' he said to himself, 'I'll have to be able to travel on land too. But how?'

He looked down at his boots, which just reached the ground. Suddenly he got an idea. He jumped off the wheelbarrow and looked under it. He tried to work out how the wheels were attached, ran back to the table and started drawing again. Once he got going again, he decided that it would be good to be able to float too. In case his travels led him to the sea.

Mr Finney stayed in the shed all night, not emerging until dawn the next day, clutching his drawings. He shuffled out, hardly able to take another step, that's how exhausted he was. He'd had a nap in a corner under an old blanket, but it had been brief and not as comfortable as in his own bed.

'Snail, wake up!' Mr Finney called after reaching his vegetable garden. Snail emerged from his house very slowly. 'What is it?' he asked sleepily.

'Snail, look at this, I've been drawing all night! I think I know how to go travelling!' Mr Finney was so excited he almost forgot how tired he was. He laid his drawings out on the ground in front of Snail.

Snail looked at them carefully.

Mr Finney couldn't wait. When would Snail say what he thought? At moments like this he wished that Snail was a bit faster. Just a little bit.

'That looks beautiful, Mr Finney,' Snail said after a long silence.

Mr Finney jumped up.

'That red thing looks complicated. Won't it be hard to make?' Snail mumbled.

Mr Finney wondered what had got into Snail. Ever since they'd met Pinky Pepper and he'd started talking about travelling, Snail had been acting strangely. Like now. After all, he knew that Mr Finney could make anything? He'd even told Pinky Pepper how clever he thought he was. Why would Snail think it was too complicated for him this time?

'No, it's not too difficult,' Mr Finney replied, turning around and striding back to the shed.

Snail was shocked. Had he said something wrong? 'Not so fast!' he shouted after Mr Finney. 'I'll come with you!'

'You just keep watch,' Mr Finney shouted back over his shoulder.

Far ahead of him, Snail saw Mr Finney pin a piece of paper on the shed door. Then he went in, slamming the door behind him. When Snail finally got closer he was able to read what was written on the piece of paper.

I'LL COME OUT WHEN I'M FINISHED. DO NOT DISTURB!

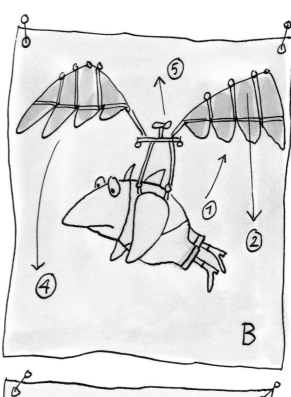

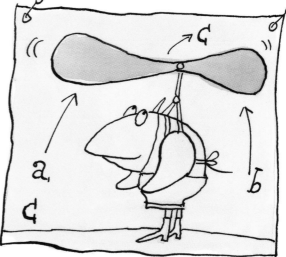

He's probably going to make that red thing, thought Snail. *And if it is difficult, it will take him a long time. I'll just keep watch.*

Snail was right: he had to wait and wait and wait. Sometimes it would be quiet for a while, then the whole shed would start shaking from the racket going on inside. The light stayed on until late at night. When Snail finally saw it switch off, he was glad that Mr Finney seemed to sleep now and then. But when he woke up in the morning, the noise inside the shed had already started again.

Snail thought a lot while keeping watch. What would happen if Mr Finney went travelling? Who could he talk to during his morning stroll? Just thinking about it made him feel sad and alone. He didn't want Mr Finney to go away. Who could change Mr Finney's mind? Pinky Pepper? No, because all she ever did was glimp from one spot to the next. Owl perhaps? He was very wise, even if he had talked to Mr Finney about travelling. *But he'd have to know he was needed here first*, thought Snail.

Slowly, very slowly, Snail started to leave a slime trail in the grass. He did nothing else. After six days he had written HELP! on the lawn in big letters.

On the seventh day Mr Finney emerged. He looked tired, but he was grinning from ear to ear. 'Thanks for keeping watch, Snail!' he said, turning back to the shed. 'Make way, here comes my invention!'

Something red and shiny drove out, almost running into Snail. Mr Finney was inside it.

'Look!' he cried. 'This is the FinMobile! It drives, it flies and it floats. And it's a submarine too!'

Snail almost fell over with surprise. His friend was even smarter than he had thought!

A proud Mr Finney showed him how the FinMobile worked. 'If you press this button,' he began, but before he'd finished his sentence they heard a familiar sound. *Frrrrrrrrrr*. It was Pinky Pepper!

'Hello, Mr Finney and Snail, how are you?' she said with the sweet smile Mr Finney had been thinking about almost every day since they met.

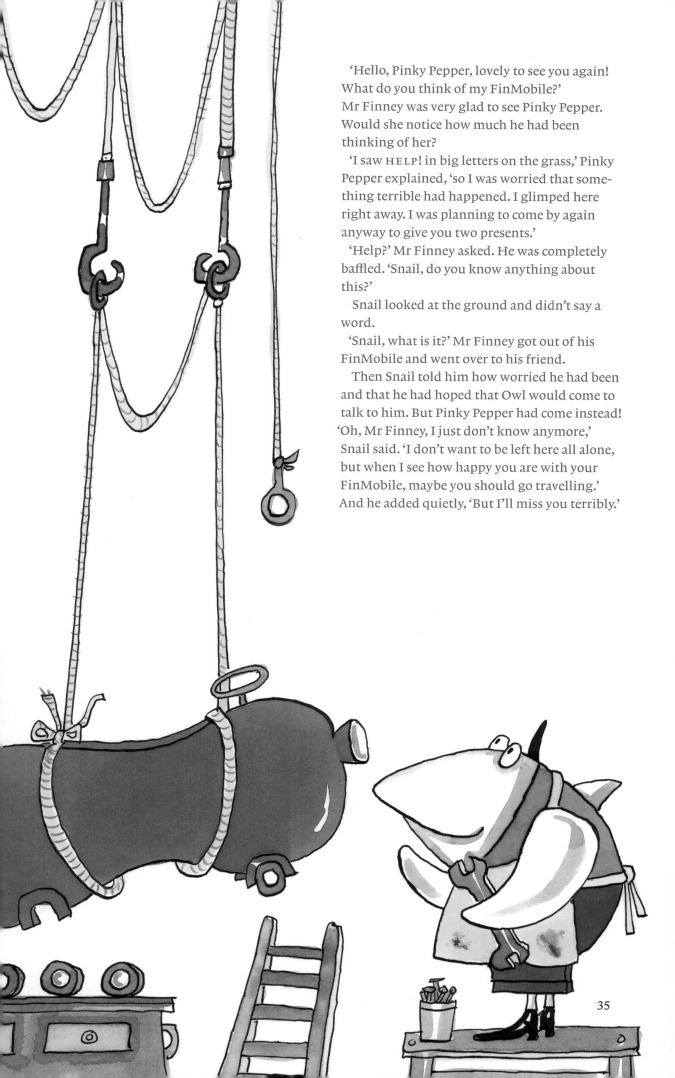

'Hello, Pinky Pepper, lovely to see you again! What do you think of my FinMobile?' Mr Finney was very glad to see Pinky Pepper. Would she notice how much he had been thinking of her?

'I saw HELP! in big letters on the grass,' Pinky Pepper explained, 'so I was worried that something terrible had happened. I glimped here right away. I was planning to come by again anyway to give you two presents.'

'Help?' Mr Finney asked. He was completely baffled. 'Snail, do you know anything about this?'

Snail looked at the ground and didn't say a word.

'Snail, what is it?' Mr Finney got out of his FinMobile and went over to his friend.

Then Snail told him how worried he had been and that he had hoped that Owl would come to talk to him. But Pinky Pepper had come instead! 'Oh, Mr Finney, I just don't know anymore,' Snail said. 'I don't want to be left here all alone, but when I see how happy you are with your FinMobile, maybe you should go travelling.' And he added quietly, 'But I'll miss you terribly.'

Mr Finney looked at Snail and felt a lump in his throat. Snail really was his best friend in the world. 'I'll miss you too, Snail,' Mr Finney whispered. 'I'll be careful and come back safely. Don't worry.'

Mr Finney walked back to the FinMobile. Pinky Pepper was standing there with one foot forwards and her hands on her sides. She looked down at the presents on the ground in front of her, then picked them up while keeping her eyes on Mr Finney.

'For you,' she said. 'I wanted to give you this in case you ever learn how to glimp.'

Mr Finney smiled.

'And now you're going travelling, it will be just what you need,' Pinky Pepper grinned.

Mr Finney unwrapped the presents. Pinky Pepper couldn't have chosen better: a backpack to carry supplies and a blue SuperBeeBee. Now he could talk with her whenever he liked, no matter where they were. He felt like giving her a kiss, but he didn't dare. 'Thank you, this is just perfect!' he said.

Snail came up now too. 'And I'll look after your house,' he said. 'That's my present.'

Mr Finney felt a warm glow come over him. He'd been sure he wanted to see the world with his own eyes, but he had never thought that he would actually manage it. Now that he was about to leave, he was a bit nervous. It wasn't an easy thing to do, especially not with Snail saying such sweet things. But there was nothing stopping Mr Finney from going travelling. He had everything he needed and his house would be well looked after. With that in mind, Mr Finney climbed into the FinMobile. 'We'll always be in touch wherever we are!' he called out to Snail and Pinky Pepper as he picked up speed.

'Always!' they shouted back. 'And have fun, wherever you go!'

The Journey

MR FINNEY had driven a long way at top speed. His eyes were watering, but that was because of the wind and had nothing to do with missing Snail and Pinky Pepper...

Now it was time to stop for a while. Mr Finney parked his FinMobile on the side of the road and got out. *Everything is different here*, he thought, looking around. At home he knew every spot and every flower. He thought of his favourite tree. Here the trees seemed to grow a lot bigger. He knew that Snail would look after his house and garden well and he was glad he didn't have to worry.

Mr Finney gazed out over the hills, where the road kept dipping down out of sight, then reappearing further away. He wondered if Pinky Pepper had ever glimpsed over this countryside. Snail would just love it here! When he saw him again he would tell him about all the things he had seen.

Mr Finney was daydreaming so much that he completely forgot where he was. No wonder he jumped when something raced past him. *Vrrrooommmmm*! A billowing cloud of dust danced over the road. What was that?

To *the* Assembly

The cloud stopped a little bit furhter down the road and Mr Finney saw a hare emerge from the settling dust. In a couple of big leaps there he was, *plop*, next to Mr Finney.

'What time is it?' the hare asked, jumping continuously from one foot to the other.

It made Mr Finney nervous, but he held out a fin to introduce himself, speaking as calmly as possible, 'I'm Mr Finney. Who are you?'

Instead of answering, the hare just repeated his question, a little hastier now, 'What time is it?'

Strange that he won't tell me who he is, thought Mr Finney.

The hare kept jumping up and down, tapping his wrist impatiently. 'I've got to get going. I'm already much too late!'

'How do you know you're late if you don't know what time it is?' Mr Finney asked.

'I'm in a hurry, that's all! You know what that is, don't you?'

'Not really. But where are you going? Would you like a ride? The FinMobile is really very fast!'

'No, thank you,' the hare said. 'I can make my own way to the assembly. Goodbye.'

'Assembly? What's an assembly? Is it fun?' Mr Finney asked.

'Fun? Fun has nothing to do with it. This is the Spring Assembly. It's very important. It's when all of the animals come together to talk about the Earth.'

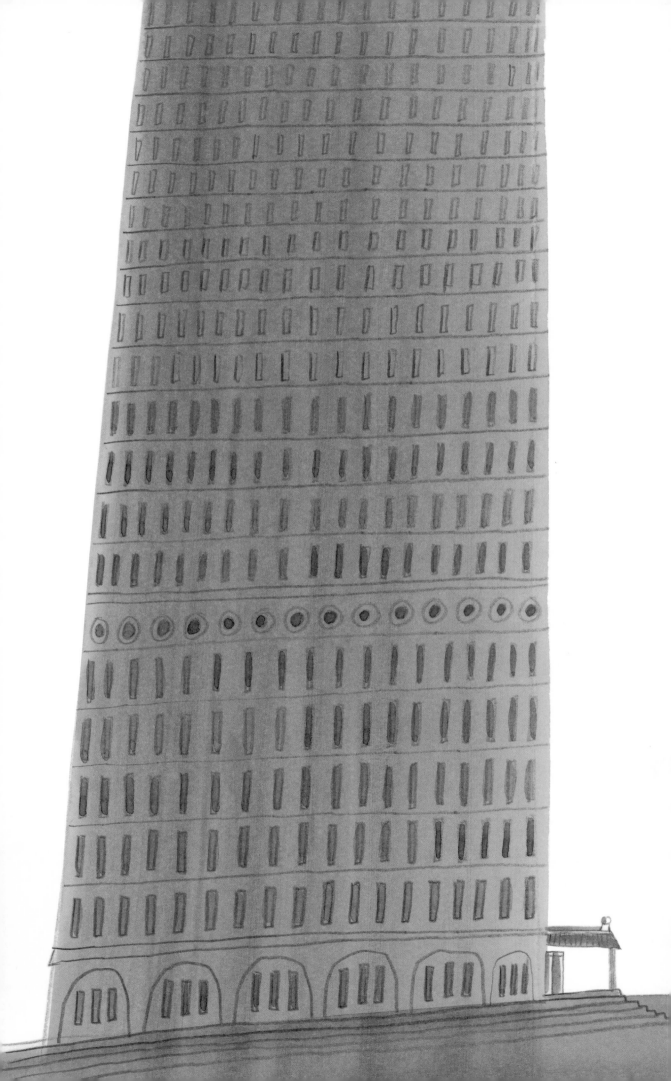

Mr Finney wanted to know whether the animals came together in summer, winter and autumn as well, but before he could ask, the hare had disappeared in a new cloud of dust.

Mr Finney thought about it. What should he do? Follow the hare to the assembly? If he wanted to discover the world he had to start somewhere! He decided to follow the hare and jumped into the FinMobile.

Mr Finney raced along after the cloud of dust. Slowly the green hills made way for the streets of a big city. Mr Finney was all eyes: it was just like the photos Pinky Pepper had shown him! It was very noisy and very crowded.

The hare stopped in front of an enormous building. Mr Finney parked the FinMobile and looked up. So many windows! He tried to count them, but there were too many and he soon lost count. Just when he was about to try again, he saw the hare disappear into the building. Mr Finney ran in after him.

In the lobby he was so surprised he immediately froze. He'd never seen a ceiling this high! Mr Finney felt very small. His mouth dropped. He walked around looking up with his head back. For a moment he forgot why he had come.

'Hey, watch where you're going!'

Mr Finney had bumped into a table. 'Oops, sorry. Accident,' Mr Finney said to the marmot that was glaring at him from behind the table.

'Are you lost or what?' grumbled the marmot.

Mr Finney looked down at the toes of his boots. 'Um, I'm looking for the hare who ran in here on his way to an assembly.'

Two beady black eyes glared at him. 'I didn't see any hare. I can't keep tabs on everyone who comes in or out, you know.'

Mr Finney swallowed and hesitated. Now what? Would he ever see the hare again?

But the marmot was helpful after all. 'Go and have a look on the twentieth floor,' he said, in a much friendlier voice. 'The lift's just over there.'

'Thank you,' Mr Finney said gratefully. Trying not to let on that he had no idea what a lift might be, he passed the marmot and knocked on a silver door.

'Don't knock,' the marmot laughed, 'you have to press the button.'

Mr Finney blushed and did as he was told, then took a deep breath when the door slowly opened. Just as he was about to step into the lift, he was almost trampled by a secretary bird carrying a black briefcase.

'Is this lift going to the twentieth floor?' Mr Finney asked. 'I have to go to an assembly.'

'Assemblies are always on the twentieth floor,' the secretary bird replied, looking down at Mr Finney and pressing the buttons marked 12 and 20.

'Are you going to the assembly too?'

The secretary bird bent forward and peered at Mr Finney through his huge glasses. His sharp beak almost jabbed him in the face. 'No, I don't like assemblies. Assemblies are for talkers, blabbermouths and chatterboxes!' He straightened his back and stared ahead silently.

When the secretary bird got out of the lift on the twelfth floor, Mr Finney wavered. He didn't like being here all alone and he didn't like not knowing where exactly he was going. Fortunately the lift stopped again quickly. This was his floor!

As the door opened Mr Finney took another deep breath and stepped forward bravely. He looked to the left and saw a long corridor with closed doors on both sides. He looked right and saw exactly the same. No, not quite: at the very end of that endless corridor one door was ajar. Could that be the Spring Assembly?

Mr Finney strode down the corridor. *Anything is better than being alone*, he thought. And he called as loudly as he dared, 'Hare, are you there? It's me, Mr Finney!'

'YOU'RE just in time,' said a small woodpecker standing at the door.

Mr Finney nodded and smiled and hoped that the woodpecker wouldn't notice that he had never been to an assembly before. If he did, he might not let him in!

The woodpecker nodded back and stepped aside to let Mr Finney in. Thank goodness! He hadn't noticed.

Looking into the room, Mr Finney saw a long table with chairs around it. On almost every chair there was an animal. He stepped closer and looked around cautiously. Suddenly he saw the hare. Mr Finney leapt with joy.

The hare happened to look in his direction, got up and hopped over to Mr Finney. 'Don't I know you from somewhere?' he asked.

'Yes, we met in the hills and I followed you to the city,' Mr Finney said quietly. 'I hope you don't mind.' Maybe the hare would tell him that he wasn't welcome here at all.

But the hare just smiled back, 'Not at all! Not at all! My name is Hare, by the way. What's yours?'

'Mr Finney,' said Mr Finney, who thought it very strange that Hare had already forgotten his name.

'Come and sit down next to me, Mr Finney,' Hare said over his shoulder as he walked back to his chair.

Mr Finney followed Hare and sat down on the empty chair next to his. Sitting across the table was a hamster, who nodded hello without speaking.

Mr Finney smiled and nodded back.

'Were you at the last assembly too?' Hare asked.

'No, this is my first time,' Mr Finney admitted. 'Is that a problem?'

'Not at all. It helps to know what we discussed last time, but most animals can't remember things that long, so we always start by repeating a lot of what was said during the Winter Assembly. It won't be a problem that you weren't here last time.'

'And you gather here to talk about the Earth,' said Mr Finney.

Hare gawked at him. 'How do you know that?'

'You told me on the side of the road.'

'Oh, now I remember! That's where we met!' Hare cried.

'Do you have a Summer Assembly and an Autumn Assembly as well?' Mr Finney asked at last.

'No Summer Assembly,' Hare said. 'In the summer a lot of animals are too busy and it's too hot for assemblies. We meet again in autumn.'

Mr Finney was about to ask another question when a loud voice made him jump. An ostrich at the head of the table announced, 'This Spring Assembly is now open!'

Empty
Forests and
Angry
Animals

'Is he in charge?' whispered Mr Finney.

'Shhh. The assembly has started. I'll explain later!' replied Hare.

'Silence!' said Ostrich. 'First I'll explain what we discussed during the Winter Assembly.'

'That's what I mean,' Hare said quietly to Mr Finney. 'It's always like that. We spend most of the time talking about the last assembly. That's why we never have time to solve any problems!'

Ostrich coughed and began. 'Last time the monkeys complained about trees being cut down in their forest. Woodpecker, refresh our memories. Why did some of us disagree with the monkeys' complaint?'

Everyone now turned to the corner of the room, where Woodpecker had sat down behind a large pile of paper.

Woodpecker began leafing through the pages. 'Some animals didn't mind the forests being cut down at all,' he said, 'because without the trees, there is more light in the forest and more room to build houses and dig burrows.'

'Thank you, Woodpecker,' said Ostrich. 'Today we have to decide what to do about the monkeys' complaint. That is why I have asked Dr Raccoon to explain what actually happens after the trees have been cut down. Then we'll at least know what we're talking about.'

A dignified-looking raccoon stood up. 'Dear delegates, it is actually very simple. If the trees are cut down, the monkeys and the other forest animals will have nowhere to live and will be unable to find enough to eat. The forest will be ruined and many animals will have to flee.'

Everyone started talking at once. 'Silence!' Ostrich said again. 'Anyone who wants to speak must raise a leg or a wing.'

An owl was the first to put up his wing. 'I live in a forest too but they aren't cutting any trees down there.'

'That's true,' answered Dr Raccoon. 'Not all forests are disappearing. But a lot more than we think are in danger. And we really need our trees. Not just to live in and get food from, but also to keep the air clean so that we can all breathe.'

Mr Finney listened carefully. He hadn't known that trees kept the air clean! 'Do you think I can ask something too?' he whispered in Hare's ear.

'Only if you think it's important,' Hare whispered back.

Mr Finney stuck up a fin. All of the animals turned to look at him. 'How do the trees keep the air clean?' he asked shyly.

'It's mainly the leaves of the trees that do it,' Dr Raccoon answered.

He took a deep breath before launching into his explanation, but before he could start speaking, Mr Finney asked another question. 'If the air is for everyone and the trees make the air clean, why doesn't everyone want to keep the trees?'

Dr Raccoon looked at Mr Finney with surprise. 'That's an important question and you're right. But unfortunately not everyone feels the same way.'

'Why not?' asked Mr Finney, who was starting to enjoy himself.

'Because it depends entirely on what's important to you!' shouted a beaver on the other side of the table. 'I live in a forest myself. I gnaw through trees and it was never a problem. Until the monkeys started to complain!' The beaver pounded the table with his fist and jumped up. 'I've had enough of it!' he yelled. He stormed out of the room, slamming the door behind him.

The animals all looked at the door with big eyes, whispering excitedly amongst themselves.

'Order!' said Ostrich. 'Um, Dr Raccoon, the table is yours.'

'I was just saying how trees keep the air clean,' Dr Raccoon continued hesitantly. 'And dirty air is something we don't want, because it covers the planet like a blanket, making it much too hot. That's why the air has to be clean and not dirty.'

'I like it when it's hot!' shrieked a parrot who was sitting diagonally opposite Hare and Mr Finney.

'And so do lots of animals,' Dr Raccoon explained. 'But if the Earth gets too hot, the ice that's on the land and in the sea in the frozen north will melt. And when it melts it will turn into so much water that it will flood over the land.'

Mr Finney couldn't believe his ears. Pinky Pepper's photos had only shown impressive forests and magnificent seas!

'It's very important that we talk about it,' Dr Raccoon continued. 'The beaver was right. How you see things depends on where you live.'

Mr Finney had to think about that for a moment. 'Like with a rainbow?' he asked hesitantly, thinking about his conversation with Snail.

Dr Raccoon nodded. 'That's a good example. You can only see a rainbow if it's raining while the sun is shining,' he said. 'And only if the rainbow...'

'We're getting off the track!' snapped Ostrich. 'Back to the forests. Who has a solution for the monkeys' problem?'

It was totally silent. Then the hamster opposite Mr Finney shouted, 'The beavers have to move!' Loud cheers went up from the other side of the table.

Ostrich shook his head. 'Sending animals away is not a solution.'

'Maybe the old chief knows,' said a petrel that had been silent up till now. 'He always listens carefully to everyone.'

'Why isn't he here anyway?' asked a meerkat, while looking around the table.

'He's not just old, he's ill too,' Ostrich replied. 'He can't make the long trip into town anymore.'

'They're talking about a famous walrus,' Hare whispered to Mr Finney. 'He lives a long way away, in the frozen north. They call him the old chief because he knows so much and always asks good questions. He's already helped solve lots of arguments and problems. But now he's ill.'

Although Mr Finney didn't understand everything everyone said, he thought the assembly was very exciting. He was glad that he had learnt something about the rainbow and he hoped to learn even more in the course of the day. 'There's actually something else I would like to ask,' he told Hare. 'Do you think it's allowed?'

'You'll have to be fast, it looks like Ostrich is about to close the assembly,' Hare said, looking at the head of the table. 'But you can never be sure with him.'

Mr Finney put up his fin.

'Another question?' Ostrich asked impatiently. 'I'm about to close the meeting!'

'It's a short question,' Mr Finney said.

'All right then,' answered Ostrich. 'But only if you keep it very short!'

Mr Finney cleared his throat. 'I don't know much about the world because I really only live in my garden with Snail and…'

'You said it would be short!' Ostrich exclaimed.

'Pinky Pepper showed me a photo of a flag on the seabed,' Mr Finney continued quickly. 'Snail and Owl and I didn't understand it, because who'd put a flag on the bottom of the sea? I was actually hoping that you might…'

'Thank you very much for this important question,' Ostrich interrupted. 'Perhaps Dr Raccoon knows the answer.'

Dr Raccoon thought for a moment. 'The old walrus once told me about an argument he tried to solve,' he said. 'The argument was about the Ice Sea in the frozen north.'

'Is that sea really that important? I mean important enough to argue about?' asked Mr Finney.

'Yes, because there are hidden treasures in the ground under the Ice Sea,' Dr Raccoon said. 'But if they dig them up, they will disturb things. And we don't want that, because lots of fish and other animals live there.'

'What's that got to do with the flag?' asked Mr Finney.

'The flag was put there by someone who thinks the treasures belong to him. But the frozen north belongs to everyone! Unfortunately the old chief is too old and too ill to find a solution. The argument might never be solved.'

The animals all looked at Dr Raccoon anxiously. Quickly Ostrich spoke up. 'Very interesting,' he said. 'Woodpecker has written everything down, so everyone can read what we said today. We'll discuss things further during the Autumn Assembly. The Spring Assembly is hereby closed!' Most of the animals got up and left the room.

'It's always like that,' Hare mumbled to Mr Finney. 'Lots of talk, very few solutions.'

'Why didn't you say something then?' asked Mr Finney.

'Ah, what's the point?' Hare answered. 'No one listens to me anyway!'

The room was almost empty. Hare too called goodbye and hopped off. *He must be on his way to something very important*, thought Mr Finney.

A Breath
of *Fresh* Air

'AND, what did you think of the Spring Assembly?' asked a crab who was standing there waiting when Mr Finney walked out of the building. 'My name is Crab.'

'I'm Mr Finney, and I thought the assembly was very exciting. It was my first time.'

'You never would have guessed. You kept on asking questions!' said Crab.

'Ostrich said that it was all right. And I always put up my fin first!' Mr Finney answered. 'What did you think of it?'

'Ah, it's always the same old story. Sometimes it's the air, sometimes it's the forests.'

'But Ostrich promised we'd look for a solution for the monkeys' problem.'

'He says that, but nothing happens. I've been warning about the sea level getting higher for years, but do you think anyone does anything about it? Of course not! That's why I just keep my mouth shut at the assemblies,' grumbled Crab.

He reminded Mr Finney of Hare, who was just as gloomy about nothing ever changing. 'But you still come to the assemblies!' Mr Finney said. 'Maybe you should ask some questions about the sea next time.'

'Ah, forget it. I'm going home. The sea air does me good. On the beach I can clear my mind.' Crab sounded more cheerful again. 'Why don't you come with me?'

Mr Finney straightened up. Sea air? Maybe that air came from the Ice Sea Dr Raccoon was talking about!

'That's very kind of you. I'd love to come with you. If you like, we can travel together in my FinMobile. But you'll have to tell me the way.'

'Gladly!' said Crab.

They got in, but it was so busy around the big building that they hardly made any headway. It was only after they had left the city far behind them that it grew quieter.

'Can I swim in the sea where you live?' asked Mr Finney.

'Sure, now that it's spring, the water has warmed up a little,' replied Crab.

Mr Finney thought of his bath at home and wondered whether the water in the sea would be very different. 'Is the sea we're going to nice?'

'I think so. But the sea can be dangerous too,' said Crab.

'Why dangerous?' asked Mr Finney with surprise.

'It's like Dr Raccoon said: when the ice melts, it puts too much water in the sea. Then the sea comes up onto the land and all the animals that live on the land have to flee.'

'Flee? But isn't that only if the forests are cut down?' Mr Finney was now totally confused. Dr Raccoon hadn't mentioned this. Maybe Crab was getting everything mixed up.

'I don't know exactly how it works either. Anyway, it's not such a problem for me, because I can swim,' Crab said. Now and then he told Mr Finney which way to go. It was starting to get dark and after a while Crab started to yawn. 'Keep going straight on,' he mumbled before closing his eyes.

Mr Finney was glad that Crab was asleep. That made it easier for him to think. If only he was back home with Snail sitting on the lowest branch of his favourite tree! He was still a bit scared of being out in the big wide world without any of his friends. But when he asked questions, he felt less alone. It worked every time: first with Hare, then with Dr Raccoon and now with Crab. But the more questions he asked, the less he seemed to understand the world.

After it grew completely dark, Mr Finney decided to park his FinMobile on the side of the road and get a bit of sleep himself. But when it started getting light again, he drove on, towards the sea.

Crab didn't wake up again until they reached the beach. Mr Finney saw the sea and danced for joy. He took a couple of deep breaths. 'You're right! The sea air is tremendous!' he shouted to Crab, who was rushing sideways towards the sea. Mr Finney pulled off his boots and let the sand tickle his toes.

When they were standing in the water, Mr Finney asked, 'Hey, Crab, why do crabs walk sideways instead of straight ahead?'

'That's just how we do it,' Crab said. 'Like you. I don't ask you why you wear those black boots, do I? And in the end we both get where we're going, don't we?'

'You're right,' Mr Finney said softly. 'I was just wondering, that's all.'

They sat next to each other and looked out to sea.

'Crab,' Mr Finney said after a while, 'where would I end up if I went into the water here? I want to go to the frozen north.'

'How are you going to do that?' Crab asked anxiously. 'Can you swim that far?'

'Don't worry about me. My FinMobile is a boat too. But I have to know where I'm going.'

'If you go straight across the sea here, you'll come to an island. I think that's still a long way from the frozen north, but you'll be going in the right direction,' Crab said.

'What's an island?' Mr Finney asked.

'That's a bit of land surrounded by water. I've heard that it's dangerous on that island, because lots of things get stolen. You'll have to be very careful of your belongings.'

Mr Finney was shocked. 'Stolen?'

'Yes, stolen. By the vultures, they say. But fortunately a lot of hamsters live there too. They're very friendly and you can trust them.'

'I was sitting opposite a hamster at the Spring Assembly. Maybe she lives on the island too,' Mr Finney said joyfully.

'That's right. But she won't have arrived yet. The trip to the island takes a long time, especially if you haven't got a FinMobile.'

Crab was silent for a moment. 'It's a shame you have to go,' he said finally. 'I've enjoyed talking to you.'

'Me too. And thanks for showing me the way to the sea. You're right, the sea air does me good!' Mr Finney skipped back to his Fin-Mobile, got in and drove cautiously towards the waves.

'Are you sure the FinMobile can float?' asked Crab.

'Definitely, if I press these buttons!' said Mr Finney proudly, pointing to four buttons with numbers on them. 'Driving is 1, sailing is 2 and flying is 3. And number 4 is for going underwater, then the FinMobile turns into a submarine. You never know!'

Mr Finney said goodbye to Crab, pressed button number 2 and plunged into the waves on his way to the island.

CRAB'S beach was soon far behind. Looking back, all Mr Finney could see was a narrow strip of land between the sea and the sky.

He had never felt this free. He was surrounded by water, water and more water. The FinMobile rolled on the waves. At first the movement gave him a strange feeling in his stomach, but he soon got used to it. 'Yippee!' he called out to no one in particular.

After a while he began to wonder just how far away the island might be. Crab had said that he needed to sail straight ahead, but how could he tell if that was what he was doing? On a road or street it was easy to see where you were going, but it wasn't the same on the water. Mr Finney started getting worried.

Suddenly he remembered the SuperBeeBee Pinky Pepper had given him. In all the excitement he'd forgotten about it! He could use it to find his way.

Mr Finney tried all of the buttons on the SuperBeeBee. It wasn't easy with the FinMobile rocking on the waves. But after a while he managed to make a map appear on the screen. The map was dark blue all over. That must be the water. He ran his fin over the map to see if he could find the island.

Dippy Daffy Dolphins

And yes, now he could see it, on the right of the screen. If he kept going straight ahead, he'd miss it completely! He turned the steering wheel to the right to get on course.

Suddenly Mr Finney heard a loud splash behind him. He spun around, but there was nothing in sight. Was it just a wave? *Splash*! This time he spotted the end of a tail sliding into the water. Dolphins! One after another they jumped up out of the water, dancing happily in the waves. Mr Finney thought it was wonderful! He was glad to have some company for a change, because the crossing was taking longer than he had expected.

'Yoo-hoo, can you hear me?' he called out to the dolphins.

Quickly they came alongside, swimming in a line next to the FinMobile, half out of the water. There were seven of them.

'Did you say something?' asked the smallest cheerfully.

'I was wondering whether you could hear me,' Mr Finney replied.

'Sure can,' said another. 'Our ears are small, but we hear you call!' They burst out laughing.

'What did you want to ask us?' said the smallest, trying to keep a straight face.

'I just wanted to say hello. I've never met fish like you before.' More loud laughter.

'We're not fish!' all seven of them said at once. 'We can't breathe underwater.'

'Sorry, I didn't know that. I'm Mr Finney, and you?'

'We're the dippy daffy dolphins!' said the biggest.

'Dippy and daffy! And double trouble!' they all shouted at once, doing backflips with a swish of their tails.

It made Mr Finney dizzy, but happy as well. And he wished that he could go swimming too. But how? He couldn't just leave his FinMobile bobbing around with the SuperBeeBee on board! What if it drifted off? Then he might never find his way back to Snail and Pinky Pepper! Of course, he could ask one of the dolphins to watch it, but he had no idea whether he could trust them. Hadn't Crab said something about things getting stolen? As much as Mr Finney longed to go swimming with the dolphins, he stayed in his FinMobile.

'What are you waiting for?' he heard behind him. 'Don't you want to join in?'

'Join in?' asked Mr Finney. 'I prefer watching you from my FinMobile.'

The dolphins disappeared, but not for long: two took turns to spiral up into the air, another did a pirouette with half its body up out of the water, four jumped over each other and the smallest pretended to walk over the water while calling out, 'Didn't you say something about a fin?''

Mr Finney looked at him with surprise. 'I said FinMobile. That's what this boat is called. And my name is Mr Finney.'

'If you've got fins, you can swim, can't you?' answered two at once. 'Or are those boots too heavy? Come on, we'll help. It'll be fun!' And before Mr Finney could say a word, the biggest of the mischievous dolphins pulled him out of the FinMobile.

'My SuperBeeBee!' shouted Mr Finney. But the smallest dolphin shouted that he needn't worry and cheerfully pushed him under.

Mr Finney was now floating in a different world. At first he couldn't see or hear a thing. He only felt the swell of the water around him. But once his eyes were used to the darkness, he saw that one of the dolphins was gesturing for him to come along. He followed the dolphin to the other six, who were constantly playing and doing tricks. At least, until the smallest got caught in cords and plastic bags that were floating in the water. He wriggled so furiously that the other dolphins only just managed to get him to the surface in time.

Mr Finney swam up quickly. 'What happened?' he asked the biggest dolphin anxiously.

'That was rubbish that's been dumped in the sea. Some animals eat it by mistake and get very sick. We've complained about it, but it didn't help. Not long ago a big school of fish went to talk to the old chief about it,' said the biggest dolphin.

'Do you mean the old walrus who lives in the frozen north?' Mr Finney asked. 'Dr Raccoon told us about him at the Spring Assembly!'

'That must be him. The fish said he tries to solve arguments. We can never go to assemblies ourselves, so we asked the old chief to go on behalf of the animals who live in the sea.'

'He wasn't at the assembly,' Mr Finney said cautiously.

'Why not?' The dolphins were clearly disappointed.

'The walrus is too old and too ill,' Mr Finney replied.

The dolphins looked at him despairingly. 'We didn't know that. Now the rubbish problem will never be solved!'

'Do you know where the walrus lives? I'd love to talk to him,' said Mr Finney.

'We've never been there. It's too cold for us. But the petrels pass the island on their way to the frozen north. They might be able to tell you more.'

'Am I going in the right direction for the island now?' Mr Finney asked, climbing back onto the FinMobile.

'Yes, you have to go straight ahead and then a bit further straight ahead. We went there once to take a hamster home,' answered one of the dolphins. 'But it's quite far. Make sure you reach the island before nightfall.'

Mr Finney nodded. 'It was great to meet you,' he said. 'And I listened carefully to what you said. You're not that dippy and daffy after all!' He started the engine, waved to his seven new friends and set a course for the island.

The sun was already low when Mr Finney saw a strip of land in the distance. He was shocked when he came closer, because in front of him a wall of white rocks rose up out of the water. How would he ever get onto the island now?

Above the rocks screeching birds floated on the wind. They were big and grey and there were lots of them. Were they the vultures Crab had warned him about? Mr Finney shivered and wondered if they were watching him. He felt very alone in his FinMobile and longed for the shelter of a nice house.

Mr Finney looked to the right and saw a wall of rocks that stretched for miles. He looked left. That way the wall looked a little lower. He decided to go left, hoping to find a place where he could climb up onto the island.

The Mysterious
Island

B LURP, *blurp*, *blurp*, went the FinMobile. It was a sound Mr Finney had never heard before. What now? He turned the engine off, then back on again. *Blurp blurp, blurp*. That didn't sound right at all! One more go, and no panicking. *Blurp, blurp, blurp*. Only now did Mr Finney see what was wrong: button number 3 was pressed when it should have been button number 2, because number 3 was for flying. 'Maybe it's time I had a little rest,' he told himself.

When Mr Finney pressed button number 2, the engine started to purr again. Slowly he sailed around the island with the white rocks. He hoped to find a sandy beach where he could get ashore easily with his FinMobile. 'There must be one somewhere,' he said out loud to raise his spirits. He closed his eyes and counted to ten while sailing on. When he opened them again, he let out a cry of joy. He'd come to the end of the rocks! It wasn't a beach though, because there were trees all the way down to the water. It was the most beautiful forest he'd ever seen!

Slowly he approached the island.

'What are you doing here?' he heard suddenly from the forest.

'Who's there?' Mr Finney asked, startled. Was it a vulture?

'What are you doing here?' the voice said again, louder this time.

'I'm trying to get up onto the island.' Mr Finney said hesitantly. Quickly he made up an excuse, 'I've come to visit a hamster I know. Who are you?'

'What's that thing you're sitting in?' the voice asked, ignoring his question.

'This is my FinMobile. But I really would find it easier to talk to you if I could see you!' Mr Finney said as calmly as he could.

'Show me who you are first. Stand up in that fin thing,' said the unfriendly voice.

'All right, but not for long. Otherwise my Fin-Mobile will start to wobble and I'll fall into the water. And I'd rather stay dry. I just went for a swim with the dolphins,' Mr Finney explained.

'Forget it then. I can see you more or less anyway. A hamster, you say? Lots of hamsters live here.'

'I met her at the Spring Assembly.'

'Oh, the Spring Assembly. A petrel told me what happened there. A friend of mine got angry and walked out.' Suddenly a brown beaver appeared from behind a big tree. 'Have you come to tell us off for cutting down trees, like at the assembly? If you have, you can just turn around again!'

'That's not why I've come,' Mr Finney explained hastily. 'I'm not just looking for the hamster. I'm also looking for the petrels who can tell me how to get to the frozen north.'

'How do I know you're not lying?' asked the beaver, peering at Mr Finney suspiciously.

'Because I'm telling the truth,' Mr Finney answered cheerfully.

The beaver was so surprised by this answer that he suddenly turned friendly. 'Sorry for asking so many questions. But I've learned to be on my guard. You can't be too careful on this island. The vultures will steal things from right under your nose.'

'I understand. The crab who lives on the beach on the opposite shore already warned me.' Mr Finney actually quite liked the beaver. 'I don't mind questions anyway. I always ask lots of questions myself.'

'Why do you have to go to the frozen north?' asked the beaver.

'Because that's where the walrus lives. He can tell me about a flag I'm looking for, a flag on the bottom of the Ice Sea.'

'What's a flag doing on the bottom of the sea?' asked the puzzled beaver.

'That's just what I want to know! It's got something to do with an argument about treasures in the seabed.'

'That sounds important. I'll help you to get onto the island, then we can talk some more,' said the beaver. 'If you sail a little bit further, you'll see a dark cave. It'll be almost underwater by now. Steer well clear of it, because strange things happen there. But past the cave there's a small bay. You can get onto the island in that bay.'

'Thank you, thank you,' Mr Finney stammered, a little worried. 'Will I see you again?'

'Sure, I'll walk to the bay and wait for you there. And it's not such a big deal. My name's Beaver.'

'I'm Mr Finney. I hope nothing happens to me on the way.'

'Don't worry. If you stay away from the cave, you'll be fine.'

'See you soon then,' Mr Finney whispered in an unsteady voice.

He did exactly what Beaver had told him to do. When he was almost at the cave he sailed a good distance out to sea to make sure he didn't come too close to it. Could there be vultures living there? Mr Finney shivered and took a deep breath before he dared to sail past. A little bit further along he saw a white crescent-shaped beach between two cliffs. What had Beaver called it again? A bay?

Mr Finney steered for the beach and pressed button 1 the moment he felt sand under the FinMobile.

'Mr Finney!' cried Beaver, who had appeared in the distance and was running towards him. 'You're here already! I'm glad it went well!'

Mr Finney raised a fin to show that he had heard Beaver.

'Look who else is here,' Beaver said when he got closer.

Mr Finney saw a hamster. She was the spitting image of the hamster he had met at the assembly.

'Beaver told me you were at the assembly,' said the hamster, holding out a paw. 'My sister was there too.'

'Is she back yet?' asked Mr Finney.

'No, not yet. It's a long journey.'

'Your sister seemed nice,' Mr Finney smiled. 'It's a shame she's not here to talk to. Your island is so beautiful!'

Beaver wasn't interested in talking about the hamster's sister. 'Hamster, do you know where Mr Finney can find the petrels?' he asked.

'The petrels?'

'Yes. They can tell me how to get to the frozen north,' Mr Finney explained.

'What do you want to go there for? They say it's cold and very far away.'

'It's a long story. Maybe I can tell you some other time.'

Hamster nodded. 'I know where the petrels rest on their way past. But we can only get there on foot. You'll have to leave that red thing here,' she said.

'Will that be okay? Won't the vultures steal my FinMobile?' asked Mr Finney, worried.

'No, not at all, it's much too big for that. Just to be on the safe side, I'll ask a couple of my nephews to check on it now and then. Come on, let's go.'

'I have to go back home,' said Beaver. 'Good luck, Mr Finney. Perhaps we'll meet again before you travel on.'

'Thanks, Beaver. You've been a great help. Maybe next time we see each other we can talk about cutting down trees,' Mr Finney laughed. Beaver grinned but didn't answer.

Hamster and Mr Finney started a long walk. Mr Finney was extremely tired, but didn't want to let it show. Hamster noticed anyway. 'Hang in there,' she said in a friendly voice. 'We're almost there.'

Mr Finney looked at the sky. 'How do we know the petrels will be there?' he asked.

'We'll only know when we see them,' Hamster replied. 'They usually rest on the northern tip of the island before making the long crossing to the frozen north. But we never know how long they're going to stay.'

As they came closer to the northern tip, Hamster started looking worried.

'Is something wrong?' asked Mr Finney.

'Um... usually they're here.'

'I can't see them anywhere.' Mr Finney tried not to sound too disappointed. After all, it wasn't Hamster's fault. 'Maybe they wanted to see the other side of the island for a change.'

'No, they always come here.' For a moment Hamster looked like she was about to cry. Her face fell and she rubbed her eyes.

'Look, there! A petrel!' Mr Finney cried. He ran as fast as he could, with Hamster just behind him.

'He's not moving,' Mr Finney said anxiously.

'Not another death,' whispered Hamster.

'What do you mean?' asked Mr Finney. 'Maybe he's just asleep.' But when he came closer he saw that Hamster was right.

'Lots of petrels eat the rubbish floating in the sea,' Hamster explained sadly. 'It's very bad for them. It kills them.'

'The dolphins told me about the rubbish and I saw it underwater with my own eyes,' Mr Finney said with a lump in his throat. He had never seen a dead animal before.

Instead of answering, Hamster started to cry. So did Mr Finney. Together they carried the petrel to a hole and covered it with sand. Then they walked all the way back to the beach in silence.

'There you are!' Mr Finney heard behind them. It was Hamster's nephews. But... where was the FinMobile? Surely this was where they had left it! Horrified, Mr Finney looked in all directions. It hadn't been stolen, had it?

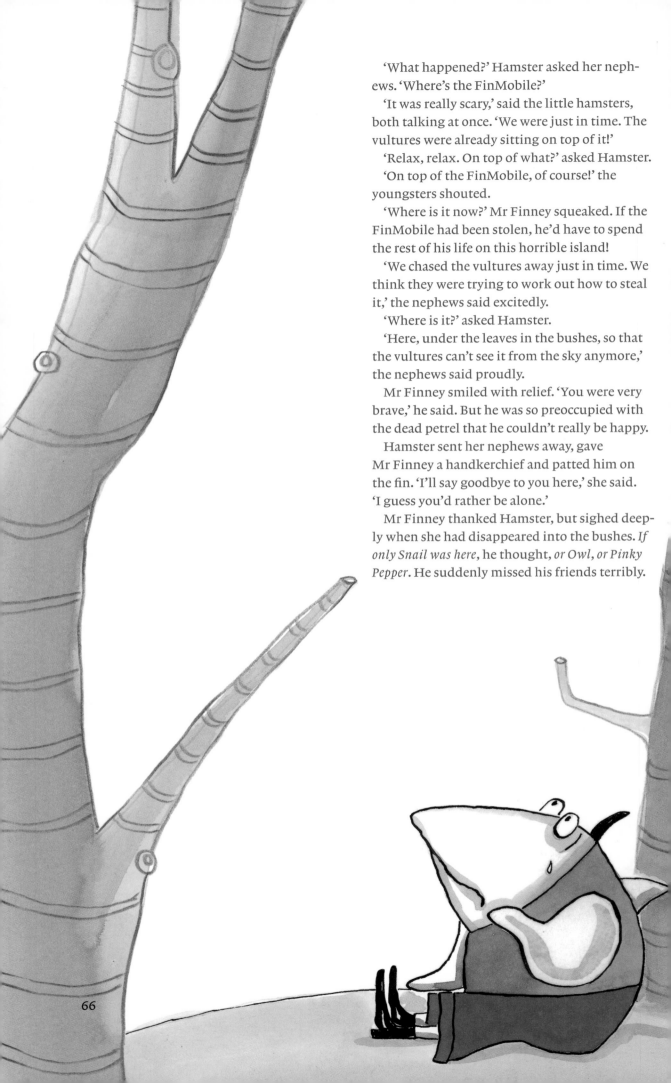

'What happened?' Hamster asked her nephews. 'Where's the FinMobile?'

'It was really scary,' said the little hamsters, both talking at once. 'We were just in time. The vultures were already sitting on top of it!'

'Relax, relax. On top of what?' asked Hamster.

'On top of the FinMobile, of course!' the youngsters shouted.

'Where is it now?' Mr Finney squeaked. If the FinMobile had been stolen, he'd have to spend the rest of his life on this horrible island!

'We chased the vultures away just in time. We think they were trying to work out how to steal it,' the nephews said excitedly.

'Where is it?' asked Hamster.

'Here, under the leaves in the bushes, so that the vultures can't see it from the sky anymore,' the nephews said proudly.

Mr Finney smiled with relief. 'You were very brave,' he said. But he was so preoccupied with the dead petrel that he couldn't really be happy.

Hamster sent her nephews away, gave Mr Finney a handkerchief and patted him on the fin. 'I'll say goodbye to you here,' she said. 'I guess you'd rather be alone.'

Mr Finney thanked Hamster, but sighed deeply when she had disappeared into the bushes. *If only Snail was here*, he thought, *or Owl, or Pinky Pepper*. He suddenly missed his friends terribly.

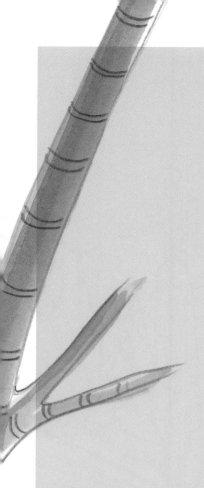

The Task

High in the Sky

M R FINNEY was totally confused. He had gone travelling to discover the world, but the more he saw, the more questions he had. He thought of home, where he could sit on the lowest branch of his favourite tree with Snail. At home everything was clear. He knew every corner of his garden. He knew exactly what grew where, when the flowers came out and when to plant new seeds. In his garden there wasn't any rubbish that killed animals and there were no arguments. Besides the arguments with the squirrels about the beechnut shells of course. But there was nowhere near as bad as here on the island. Here petrels died and everyone was scared of the vultures, who stole everything.

Mr Finney was scared and sad and lonely. 'I'm not going to cry, am I?' he whispered to himself. But that didn't help. He sniffed and swallowed. Now it was really getting dark. How could he protect himself and the FinMobile from the vultures in the night?

Suddenly he knew what to do. He had to ask Pinky Pepper to come to him! After all, Pinky Pepper was able to glimp, she could get to him in a flash.

He got his SuperBeeBee out of the FinMobile and wrote a message, a message that was as cheerful as possible, so as not to worry Pinky Pepper. After a few attempts he managed to send it. Mr Finney sighed. Now he just had to wait.

Frrrrrrrrrrr, he felt, much sooner than he had hoped. Mr Finney looked up and turned his head left and right as fast as he could. He looked behind him. He recognised the sound and the sensation. Had she really received his message? *Frrrrrrrrr*. Yes, he was sure of it, here she was! Mr Finney stood up straight and tried to smile. He didn't want her to see that he was actually very sad. *Frrrrrrrrrrrr*. There she was in front of him, fluttering her lashes.

'Mr Finney, how nice to see you!' called Pinky Pepper.

'I'm glad you got my message!' answered Mr Finney. His voice sounded different from usual, a bit shaky.

'What's the matter?' asked Pinky Pepper.

Mr Finney looked into her gleaming eyes. 'I'm not happy, Pinky Pepper,' he said softly. 'I am totally confused. I went travelling because I wanted to discover the world. And there is a lot to discover. But there are so many problems that are too big and too sad for me to get my head around. Maybe I should just go back home.'

'Back home? Mr Finney, you mustn't! My brave Finney, giving up at the first setback?'

Mr Finney looked up. Pinky Pepper had called him brave! He felt better already and straightened his back. 'You're right. Of course I won't give up,' he mumbled uncomfortably.

'What did you say?' Pinky Pepper asked. 'Did you say you're not giving up? See, you know what to do! You just have to say it louder, "I am not giving up!"'

Nobody can stay sad for long with someone as cheerful as Pinky Pepper around, thought Mr Finney.

'Let's do it together on the count of three,' she chattered on. 'One, two, three!'

'I am not giving up!' they screamed into the wind, Pinky Pepper a little louder than Mr Finney.

Mr Finney couldn't help but chuckle.

'See? It really helps,' Pinky Pepper said. 'A little yell now and then is a great relief!'

They sat down on the sand and looked out over the sea, which was glittering in the light of the moon and the stars.

'So, tell me about your travels,' Pinky Pepper said after a long silence. 'Try to explain what's got you confused.'

'If they cut down the trees,' Mr Finney began, 'then the animals who live in the forest won't have a home anymore and they'll have to flee. But they still cut down the trees!'

'That's not good,' Pinky Pepper said quietly.

Mr Finney continued, 'And if they dig up the treasures in the Ice Sea, it will disturb everything and the fish and the other animals won't be able to live there anymore. But someone's still put a flag on the bottom of the sea to show everyone that the treasures belong to him.'

Pinky Pepper shook her head in disbelief.

'Living in the frozen north is an old walrus who's supposed to be even wiser than Owl,' Mr Finney went on. 'He's already solved lots of problems, but now he's too ill and too old. I wanted to go see him to ask my questions, but the only petrel that could have shown me the way to the frozen north died from eating rubbish that had been dumped in the sea.'

Before Mr Finney could get sad again, Pinky Pepper began fluttering excitedly back and forth in front of him. 'I know where it is. I've been there before,' she blurted. 'In the frozen north. It was really cold.'

Mr Finney leapt for joy. Pinky Pepper could help him! Maybe she would even come with him!

It was as if Pinky Pepper could read his mind. 'You know what, I'll come with you,' she said. 'After all, it's a lot more fun to do things together than alone.'

Mr Finney beamed. 'Unfortunately I can't glimp,' he said, 'but we could fly to the frozen north in the FinMobile!'

They dragged the FinMobile out of the bushes and climbed in. 'I hope it's not too cold for us high up in the sky,' Pinky Pepper sighed.

'I thought of that!' Mr Finney said, pressing a couple of buttons next to the steering wheel. A transparent bubble appeared and closed over their heads like a fishbowl.

'But how does the FinMobile know that it has to fly and not drive?' Pinky Pepper asked.

'With this!' Mr Finney said, pressing button number 3. 'Driving is 1, sailing is 2 and flying is 3. And number 4 turns it into a submarine,' he explained. 'For when we find the flag.'

'He's really thought of everything. What a hero,' said Pinky Pepper, whispering so quietly that Mr Finney couldn't hear her.

'Fasten your seatbelts!' called Mr Finney. He pressed the red start button and slowly pushed the steering wheel forward. The FinMobile started thrumming and rolling forwards. Gleaming wings folded out on both sides. 'Here we go!' shouted Mr Finney. The FinMobile's wheels came up off the ground.

'How exciting!' yelled Pinky Pepper once they were high up in the air.

'You're not airsick?' Mr Finney asked anxiously.

Pinky Pepper shook her head and laughed. 'Flying in your FinMobile is fantastic!'

They flew all night, until the sun slowly rose. 'Are we still going the right way?' asked Mr Finney.

Pinky Pepper got out her SuperBeeBee and looked from the screen to the ground and back again. 'I think so. I can only see snow,' she said.

Mr Finney spotted something. 'Look, look!' He pointed down. 'Do you see that gleaming white building? It looks like it's made of glass! Who do you think lives there?'

'That must be the old chief's palace!' Pinky Pepper cried. 'Yes, that's it. It's an ice palace!'

'Then it's time to land!' Mr Finney pressed a button that made the FinMobile fly lower. The engine roared.

'Do you see how big that palace is?' Mr Finney asked.

'What?' Pinky Pepper shouted.

'Do you see how big that palace is?' Mr Finney yelled. 'And it's so beautiful here! The ice looks like silver!'

They both bounced on their seats when the FinMobile landed. Then Mr Finney opened the roof so they could climb out. They both had a good stretch.

'It's so quiet here,' Mr Finney said. 'As if no one lives here.'

Pinky Pepper didn't reply. She was staring open-mouthed at the ice palace. It looked like a glittering diamond.

In the Ice Palace

MR FINNEY and Pinky Pepper couldn't believe their eyes. The ice palace had looked magnificent from above, but only now did they see how special it really was.

Together they slid over the snow to the big entrance at the front. As there wasn't a bell, Pinky Pepper knocked politely on the icy front door.

A little later a beak appeared. 'Who is it?'

'Pinky Pepper and Mr Finney,' said Mr Finney. 'We've come to see the old chief. We know he's ill, but it's very important.'

'Do you have an appointment?' asked the voice.

'I don't believe so,' Mr Finney said. 'But we do have a question. Is that okay?'

The door now opened all the way and a petrel emerged. 'No appointment, but a question,' he mumbled. 'Hmmmm. I'll have to ask.' He pressed a few buttons on a telephone that was mounted next to the door. 'Me here,' he said. 'Can I speak to the old chief for a moment?' He stared at Mr Finney and Pinky Pepper silently. 'Yes, two of them,' he said after a while. 'Mr Pinney and Finky Fepper...'

Pinky Pepper giggled, but didn't say anything.

The petrel laid a wing over the receiver and bent forward. 'The old chief wants to know where you come from.'

'From very far away. I live in a house with a garden. We've travelled far to come here,' said Mr Finney.

'And I come from everywhere and nowhere,' smiled Pinky Pepper.

The petrel repeated their answers in the receiver. 'Yes,' he said, 'a question, they have a question.' He listened for a moment, then looked at them intently while asking, 'What's the question about?'

'We'd rather explain that to him ourselves,' replied Mr Finney. 'But it's very important.'

Mr Finney and Pinky Pepper heard a deep growl from the telephone.

'Certainly,' the petrel said. 'I'll bring them to you.'

They followed the petrel down endless ice corridors. The only sound was the shuffling of their own feet on the slippery floor. But suddenly Pinky Pepper yelped.

'Careful!' called Mr Finney.

Too late! Pinky Pepper had slipped and landed hard on her bottom.

'Ouch!'

'Shhhh,' said the petrel, looking back with an annoyed expression.

Mr Finney helped Pinky Pepper up and took her by the hand. They walked on more cautiously until the petrel stopped in front of a big door.

'This is it,' he whispered. 'Remember, the old chief is ill. You can't talk to him for too long.'

Pinky Pepper smoothed her skirt and straightened the bow in her hair. She looked at Mr Finney and brushed his fin with her hand. 'We have to look respectable,' she said quietly. 'It's not every day we meet a wise old chief.'

Mr Finney nodded nervously. He could hardly wait to meet the walrus, but he was a bit scared too.

The petrel knocked on the door and swung it open.

Mr Finney and Pinky Pepper looked into a big room with a high-backed sofa in the middle and a wooden chest in the corner. That was all.

The petrel waved them in and closed the door.

Cautiously Mr Finney and Pinky Pepper walked around to the other side of the sofa. The first thing they saw were two brown flippers plunged into a big tub of steaming water.

'The older I get, the more I feel the cold,' said a deep voice. The walrus was lying on one side and leaning on a wooden stick. His tusks were curled back and almost poking into his old body. 'But I'm sure you haven't come to talk about my cold flippers,' he said. 'Welcome. Come a little closer. I don't know you, but I'm glad to see you. It's been a long time since someone came to ask me something.'

Mr Finney cleared his throat. He realised that he didn't have a lot of time to explain why they had come. He could see for himself that the walrus was old and ill. 'This is Pinky Pepper and I'm Mr Finney,' he said hurriedly. 'We're glad to meet you too. I live very far from here in a house with a garden. I know its every nook and cranny. But then Pinky Pepper showed up with all kinds of photos of things I'd never seen and I wanted to go travelling. My friend Snail didn't want me to, but Owl said I should. Then I built the Fin-Mobile. I wanted to see the forests and oceans with my own eyes. But now I know that the forests are being cut down and the oceans are full of rubbish. And I don't really understand why.' He stopped for a moment to catch his breath. 'There was one photo of a flag on the seabed. Dr Raccoon says that you know what that flag's doing there. And that's why we've come. To ask you questions.'

The walrus gave a deep sigh. 'Well,' he began slowly, 'everyone has questions. There are so many things we want to know. Simple things, like how old someone is or what they're called. But complicated things too, like how many stars there are in the sky and what happens to the moon when the sun rises.'

77

These were the very questions Mr Finney had asked himself so often! He was glad he'd come to see the old chief.

'And you might want to know why we don't fall off the Earth and who the Earth belongs to and who should look after it,' the walrus continued.

'Yes, exactly!' said Mr Finney. It was as if the walrus could read his mind.

'You know, there's nothing wrong with not understanding everything,' the walrus mumbled. 'As long as you keep asking questions and do your best. And never forget that the solutions are often closer than you think.'

It was quiet for a moment. Mr Finney and Pinky Pepper didn't dare speak. All they could hear was the splash of the flippers in the water, which had almost stopped steaming.

'My body is worn out,' the walrus groaned. His face twisted with pain as he pulled his flippers up out of the water. 'I'm so old that I don't have long to live.'

Mr Finney thought of the dead petrel he and Hamster had buried.

'Who'll be the chief when you're gone?' Pinky Pepper asked quietly.

'That's a good question,' the walrus answered. He pounded the ice floor three times with his wooden stick. A moment later the door swung open. An elegant bird stepped in and bowed.

Mr Finney looked at Pinky Pepper with surprise. She was beaming with joy. Before he could ask why, he'd figured it out: the bird was a flamingo! A pink flamingo! Pinky Pepper's favourite colour!

'This is Flingo,' the old chief said after a while. 'When I'm gone, he'll travel the world solving problems, the way I used to.'

If he's the new chief, thought Mr Finney, *Pinky Pepper might not like me as much anymore. Because he's pink and I'm not.*

Pinky Pepper stood with her hands behind her back and one foot forward, looking down shyly.

Mr Finney thought she was being quite silly. That wasn't why they had come! 'Dr Raccoon said that you'd tried to solve an argument not far from here, in the frozen north,' he said to the walrus. 'An argument about a flag.'

The walrus nodded. 'The argument started when the vultures put a flag on the floor of the Ice Sea. After that they thought the sea and the treasures in the seabed were theirs. The other animals were furious.'

'Which animals?' asked Mr Finney.

'The fish and the polar bears amongst others,' answered the walrus. 'They were very angry when they discovered the flag. They're scared that when the vultures dig the treasures up out of the seabed, they'll disturb things here forever. And that animals will no longer be able to live there.'

Before he could say anymore, he was overcome by a coughing fit that seemed to go on forever. Mr Finney, Flingo and Pinky Pepper exchanged anxious glances.

'I'm afraid you'll have to go now,' the walrus said after he'd caught his breath. 'I'm too ill to talk anymore. But before you leave, I'd like to give you something.' He pointed at the big wooden chest in the corner of the room with his stick.

Flingo opened the chest and got out an envelope, which he brought over to the old chief.

'This was actually meant for just Flingo,' the walrus coughed. 'But your question has a lot to do with its contents. So the envelope is now for all three of you.'

Mr Finney and Pinky Pepper bent forward to hear his words.

'Who shall I give it to?' asked the walrus.

A fin went up into the air.

'Mr Finney,' the old chief whispered. 'There are two important tasks in this envelope. Open it together with Flingo and promise me that you will carry them out.'

Mr Finney gave his solemn promise.

'Go now. I have to sleep,' the walrus panted. He lay down, closed his eyes and sighed deeply.

Flingo, Pinky Pepper and Mr Finney tiptoed out of the room sadly, closing the door very quietly behind them. The walrus really was deathly ill.

'This way,' the petrel whispered, 'I'll show you out.'

'Asking questions and doing your best,' Mr Finney mumbled to himself as they walked through the ice palace's long halls. And he kept repeating the walrus's wise words until they reached the doors and said goodbye to the petrel, 'Solutions are often closer than you think.'

An
Important
Envelope

FLINGO and Mr Finney walked over to the FinMobile, where Pinky Pepper was already fidgeting on the back seat.

'Climb in, Flingo,' she giggled. 'There's plenty of room for three.'

'That's right,' said Mr Finney in a surly voice. 'But does anyone know where we're going?'

'I think we'll find out when we open the envelope,' said Flingo, climbing into the FinMobile.

Mr Finney got in too. Before starting the engine he passed the envelope to Flingo.

'Quick, open it. I want to know what's inside!' said Pinky Pepper, leaning forward from the back seat and trying to snatch the envelope.

But Flingo was too fast for her. 'Careful, careful!' he laughed. 'We have to take good care of it!' He pulled out a pocketknife, opened it and slowly cut open the flap of the envelope.

'Show me, show me!' Pinky Pepper shouted excitedly.

Very carefully, as if holding something very fragile, Flingo pulled out a letter, unfolded it and began to read.

'This envelope contains two important tasks. Follow the map carefully for the first task. Look after them carefully, take them to the right place and put them in the ground. For the second task, go to the heart of the argument and say: the sea belongs to everyone, take good care of it!'

Flingo passed the letter to Pinky Pepper.

'What do we have to look after?' she asked.

'This,' Flingo said, pulling out a small bag tied with a string. 'These are seeds that can grow into trees.'

'Look! There's something else in the envelope!' Pinky Pepper exclaimed, pulling out a crumpled piece of paper.

'That's the map we need for the first task,' explained Flingo.

Pinky Pepper gave him the map.

'See that red cross? That's even further into the frozen north. I think that's where we have to take the seeds.'

'To the frozen north?' Mr Finney asked with surprise. 'At home in my garden they grow best when the sun is shining!

'They're not supposed to grow,' Flingo said. 'The frozen ground will preserve them. Then if it ever happens that there aren't any trees left in the world, we can go and get the seeds.'

'No trees left in the world?' Pinky Pepper didn't understand at all, but suddenly it was clear to Mr Finney.

'Lots of trees have already disappeared. The monkeys were complaining about that at the Spring Assembly,' he explained, 'because the animals who live in the forest have to find a new place to live.'

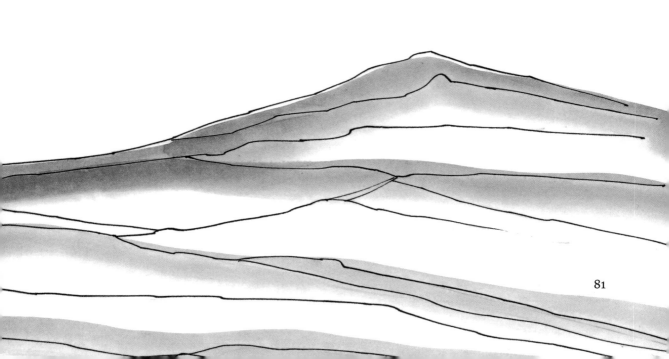

'Shall we go there as fast as we can?' Flingo suggested.

Mr Finney nodded. He pressed button number 3 and shouted over the noise, 'Seatbelts on!' And off they went, high into the sky.

The further north they went, the colder it got. Pinky Pepper and Flingo looked out breathlessly as they flew over jagged white mountains. It was magical! Now and then, they saw flocks of petrels flying past.

Slowly the sky turned orange red. When the sun was a ball of fire just above the horizon, they saw a building in the distance.

Pinky Pepper looked at her SuperBeeBee. 'It looks just like the old chief's map! I think we're almost there!' she called cheerfully.

Mr Finney flew down lower and landed the FinMobile gently on the ground.

Pinky Pepper jumped out and fluttered around. 'Look,' she exclaimed. 'There's someone in a long coat standing at the door!'

Whoever it was had their back turned and they couldn't make out a face. They hesitated. 'I'll go first,' said Flingo finally.

Mr Finney and Pinky Pepper followed a few steps behind. 'What are you doing here?' they heard a hoarse voice say.

The figure in the coat still had its back half turned to Flingo.

'We're here to deliver something important,' said Flingo. 'Something that needs to be looked after very well. A bag of seeds from the wise old chief.'

Suddenly Mr Finney nudged Pinky Pepper. 'Oh, no! That's a vulture!' he whispered. 'Vultures are thieves. They tried to steal my FinMobile!'

Pinky Pepper knew immediately what to do. 'Quick!' she whispered. 'We have to make sure Flingo doesn't give him the seeds!'

Mr Finney and Pinky Pepper came up alongside Flingo.

'Just give the bag to me,' said the vulture. 'It's in good hands here!'

Flingo was about to give it to the vulture when Pinky Pepper stepped forward, holding out a hand for the vulture to shake.

Flingo was too surprised to speak.

'Hi, I'm Pinky Pepper,' she said cheerfully to the vulture. 'Isn't it beautiful here!'

He scowled at her. 'This is all ours,' he said. 'Our snow and our ice floes. And, of course, our Ice Sea, of which we're so proud!'

'Has it always been yours?' asked Mr Finney.

'Who cares?' the vulture snapped. 'It's ours now!'

Flingo turned pale. He began to realise that giving the seeds to the vulture wasn't such a good idea!

'But how did you make it yours?' Pinky Pepper asked in her most charming voice.

The vulture went over next to her and whispered something in her ear.

Pinky Pepper squinted and held a hand up to her ear, pretending she couldn't understand. 'What's that?' she said. 'A flag? A flag on the bottom of the sea?'

'That's right,' the vulture said proudly. 'We put it there. Now everyone knows that the Ice Sea and its hidden treasures belong to us!'

It is exactly as the walrus said, Mr Finney thought, getting very annoyed. *The vultures have started the fighting over the Ice Sea!*

'How fabulous, a flag on the bottom of the sea,' Flingo told the vulture while winking at Mr Finney. 'Extraordinary! I've always wanted to see something like that!'

Mr Finney and Pinky Pepper realised that Flingo was trying to trick the vulture.

The vulture beamed with pride.

'Then you'll show us the flag?' asked Pinky Pepper, turning her sweetest face towards him.

The vulture looked at them. 'All right,' he said after a while. 'But only if you give me the bag of seeds first.'

Pinky Pepper was unstoppable. 'Of course,' she said. 'But can't we just have a peek at the flag first? And you really must tell me everything about how you put the flag there. I think it was so clever of you!' She fluttered her lashes again.

'We can go there in my FinMobile,' Mr Finney offered.

The vulture hesitated. He was on guard duty at the grey building. Was it okay for him to leave his post to show the visitors the flag in exchange for the bag of seeds?

Mr Finney put an end to his pondering. He had walked over to the FinMobile and started the engine. 'Get in,' he told Flingo and Pinky Pepper. Then he asked the vulture, 'Do you mind flying above us to show us the way?' Cautiously he steered the FinMobile over the ice.

Reluctantly the vulture flew ahead of the FinMobile. After a very long time he gradually started to fly lower. 'Stop,' he called down. 'This is it! So give me the bag!'

They'd stopped at a hole in the ice.

Pinky Pepper recognised it. She'd glimpsed here once before. She whispered something in Mr Finney's ear and Mr Finney whispered something in Flingo's ear.

Mr Finney had his fin ready on button number 4 while Pinky Pepper climbed out of the FinMobile. The transparent bubble came out again and almost closed.

Pinky Pepper fluttered over to the vulture and asked with a smile, 'Aren't you ever cold?'

The vulture growled something they couldn't make out.

'Would you like to feel how cold my hands are?' She held them both out.

The vulture blushed and stepped closer.

Frrrrrrrrrrrr. Pinky Pepper was gone!

The vulture turned around just in time to see the FinMobile disappear through the hole in the ice.

84

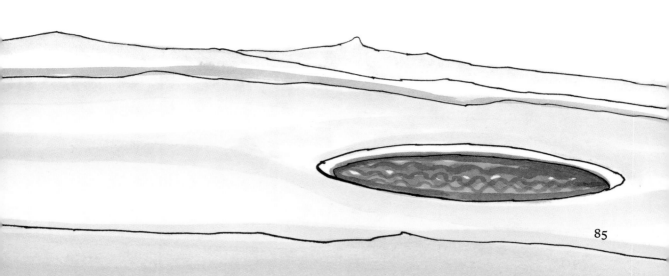

PINKY PEPPER pressed her nose against the transparent bowl. Only now did she believe that the FinMobile could go underwater as well as float, fly and drive! 'I'm good at glimping,' she told Mr Finney, 'but no one can match you when it comes to building FinMobiles!'

Mr Finney beamed. At last Pinky Pepper had said something nice about him again!

'Look!' Flingo exclaimed. He was pointing at something yucky floating in the water.

'That's rubbish,' Mr Finney told him. 'The dolphins get caught in it and the petrels can even die from it.'

Flingo looked worried. 'The wise old chief wanted to have a meeting with all the animals that live in and on the sea to find a solution for the rubbish,' he said.

'Did he?' Mr Finney asked hopefully.

'No, much to his disappointment. He's even worried that the fish and polar bears might have to flee now that the vultures are bossing everyone around in the frozen north. The vultures only think of themselves.'

'I kind of understand the vultures,' said Pinky Pepper softly.

'What?' exclaimed Flingo.

'How can you say that?' Mr Finney asked.

'Maybe the vultures just don't think things through,' Pinky Pepper replied. 'If you don't think about things or ask questions, you can do stupid things by accident.' She looked very unhappy. 'Sometimes I don't think about the things I see either.'

'Don't take it to heart, Pinky Pepper,' Mr Finney said in a friendly voice. 'You can learn to ask questions. And you've got friends who love you just as you are.'

'Thank you, Mr Finney,' Pinky Pepper whispered, smiling a little.

Suddenly Mr Finney found the courage to speak up. 'I live in a lovely house with a beautiful garden. Why don't you come and live with me?' he suggested. 'I'm sure Snail would love to have you too!'

'I like you and Snail very much, Mr Finney, but I couldn't live in just one spot,' Pinky Pepper said sadly. 'If I couldn't glimp all over the world, I'd die of boredom.'

Mr Finney was so shocked that he stalled the FinMobile. He didn't want Pinky Pepper to die!

Flingo laid a reassuring wing on Mr Finney's fin. 'If you let Pinky Pepper do what she likes best, she'll live a long, happy life,' he said. 'And you don't have to live together to be friends forever, do you?'

Mr Finney nodded, started the engine and steered silently down. Flingo and Pinky Pepper were quiet too.

Deeper they went and deeper still. The deeper they went, the darker it grew.

'We can't stay under water too much longer,' Pinky Pepper said. 'Once the sun has set, we won't see a thing anymore.'

Flingo pulled out a torch and aimed the beam of light through the water.

'Look, there, part of a ship!' Pinky Pepper pointed. 'How exciting!'

Writing *in the*

Snow

'Maybe that ship sunk looking for the flag too,' said Flingo.

'I see something shining!' Mr Finney cried suddenly. 'Look!'

Now Pinky Pepper and Flingo could see it too. There, on the seabed, stood an enormous flag. It didn't flutter or drift. It stood there perfectly still. Whenever the torch caught it, it flashed.

'The walrus said it's made of metal,' Flingo said.

They circled the flag for a while, looking at it from all sides.

'It looks even stranger than in the photo,' said Pinky Pepper.

'How did you take the photo?' Mr Finney asked. 'Can you glimp underwater too?'

Pinky Pepper shook her head. 'A seal took it for me with my SuperBeeBee,' she said. 'I couldn't hold my breath long enough and it's too deep and cold for me to swim here anyway!'

Meanwhile Flingo had picked up the important envelope. He unfolded the sheet of paper and read the tasks once again. 'We have to let the animals know that the sea belongs to everyone and that we have to look after it well,' he said.

'Then we'll start by pushing the flag over,' said Mr Finney, 'so the fish know that the vultures aren't in charge around here!'

Flingo and Pinky Pepper thought that was an excellent idea.

Mr Finney steered the FinMobile until it was just nudging the flag, then carefully accelerated. It took a while for anything to happen, but gradually the flag started to tilt and in the end it fell over on the seabed with a dull thud.

Flingo cheered and a delighted Pinky Pepper slapped Mr Finney on the back.

'Back up to the surface, fast!' she said. 'While there's still light to help us find the hole in the ice.'

Slowly the FinMobile started to rise. The journey up took a long time and it got darker and darker.

'There's the hole!' cried Pinky Pepper.

Relieved, Mr Finney steered the FinMobile towards it. 'Now we have to let the vultures know that the sea belongs to everyone,' he said. Suddenly he thought of Snail, who had written HELP on the lawn in his garden. 'And I know just how to do it,' Mr Finney said proudly.

A little later the FinMobile popped up through the hole in the ice. As it was already dark, they started straight away: treading down the snow as they worked from left to right. When they were finished and looked at the result from a distance, Pinky Pepper gave a little shriek, 'We've forgotten the A in sea and the space between THE and SEA!'

Mr Finney noticed it now as well. It said THESE BELONGS TO EVERYONE. Terrible! How could they have made a mistake like that at such an important moment?

They sighed and started again a little further along. And this time they got it right. THE SEA BELONGS TO EVERYONE was written in the snow in big letters. Mr Finney quickly added an exclamation mark at the end.

'Why are you writing that?' they suddenly heard from the sky. 'And where are my seeds?' The vulture who had brought them here was circling menacingly over their heads.

'Thank you very much for leading us to the hole in the ice,' Flingo said politely. 'You really do care about the frozen north and its treasures, just like all the other vultures.'

The vulture looked surprised. He wasn't used to being thanked for anything.

'But the ice and sea are also important to the other animals who live here,' Flingo continued. 'The sea belongs to them just as much as it belongs to you. The fish and the other animals want to look after it together with the vultures.'

'If that's true,' the vulture asked mistrustfully, 'why hasn't anyone ever told us? The fish only ever yell at us and the polar bears only come to argue!'

'See!' Pinky Pepper exclaimed. 'The vultures have just never thought it through!'

Flingo began to realise that she might be right. 'Maybe you would like to talk to the fish and listen to the polar bears?' he asked in a friendly voice. 'Then the animals that live in the sea can explain how important their home is to them.'

The vulture nodded. No one had ever been so friendly to him before! He tried to hide how moved he was by turning his back and flying off.

But Mr Finney had noticed. 'He listened to us!' he cried happily.

'The walrus will be so happy!' Flingo cried. 'I'm going to go tell him straightaway!'

Mr Finney stood there hesitantly. 'Um, Flingo, I really would like to go home now,' he said cautiously.

'Don't worry about me,' Flingo said, spreading his wings. 'I'm quite capable of flying to the ice palace myself.'

Only now did Mr Finney see how big he was.

'Pinky Pepper,' Flingo said, 'I am truly glad to have met you.' He bent forward to give her a kiss.

Pinky Pepper's red cheeks clashed with her pink dress. She fluttered her lashes. 'I'll glimp your way sometime,' she said softly.

'And I'll never forget you either,' Flingo told Mr Finney. 'Make sure you remember all you've seen and heard when you're home again.'

Mr Finney nodded and shook Flingo's wing. 'I don't know how to thank you,' he said softly. 'But come and visit sometime. You're always welcome.'

'I'll do that,' Flingo said. 'Bye!' He took a run-up and slowly took off.

Pinky Pepper and Mr Finney watched him until he was out of sight. They knew that the time had come for them to say goodbye to each other. Mr Finney took a deep breath, but before he could say a word, Pinky Pepper disappeared in a cloud of pink glitter. He felt a *Frrrrrrrrrrrrrrrrrrr* and she was gone. He stared out over the white plain, but Pinky Pepper didn't come back. He was missing her already.

Climbing into the FinMobile, Mr Finney knew that it would be a long trip. He started the engine, did up his seatbelt and pressed button number 3. The wings folded out and the Fin-Mobile took off, rising higher and higher, up above the clouds.

Suddenly his SuperBeeBee beeped. He had a message! Mr Finney looked at it and smiled. Slowly a tear rolled down his cheek. He read, 'It was hard to say goodbye. But I think you're very sweet. Forever yours, Pinky Pepper.'

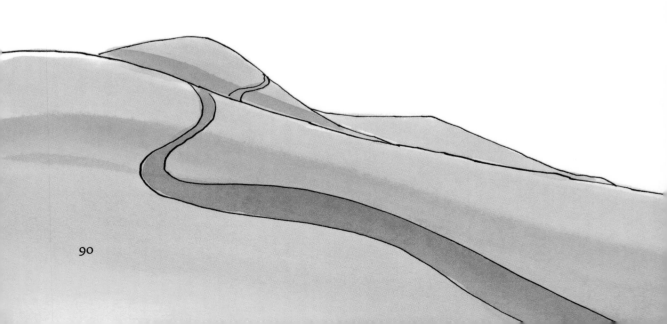

MR FINNEY flew his FinMobile as if he'd been doing it his whole life. He looked down over endless clouds and up at a sky full of stars. His SuperBeeBee showed him the way home. He was looking forward to sleeping in his own bed and could hardly wait to tell Snail about his adventures.

Suddenly Mr Finney saw a bag lying on the seat next to him. It was the bag of seeds the walrus had given them! Mr Finney was shocked. The old chief had entrusted them with the task of burying the seeds in a good place! Mr Finney put the seeds in his pocket. What should he do now?

He was still worrying about it when he saw something familiar beneath him. Those hills... Weren't they the hills around his garden? He flew a bit lower and recognised more and more. And when the sun came up, he took another look. Now, he was absolutely certain: he was home!

Mr Finney descended and landed the FinMobile softly on the lawn. After the FinMobile stopped, he retracted the wings and climbed out. He did it very slowly, one foot after the other, because he was too happy to let the moment pass quickly.

Everything was the same, but things were still slightly different. His favourite tree swayed softly in the breeze.

An Unexpected Place

The plants in his vegetable garden were in flower. The garden gate was open and the sun was shining on the water barrel. And there, on the path, beechnut shells were spread hither and thither. He had almost forgotten his argument with the squirrels. But his tree and his house looked smaller than when he left. 'Or could I have grown?' mumbled Mr Finney.

'You're back!' he heard behind him.

Mr Finney turned around. 'Snail!' he called cheerfully. 'I've missed you!'

'It's so good to see you again!' said Snail. 'You have to tell me everything that's happened. And is everything going to be the same as before?'

Mr Finney had to laugh. 'You haven't changed a bit,' he said. 'Shall we have a cup of tea and a biscuit?'

Together they walked into Mr Finney's house. Once they were sitting down, Mr Finney told Snail about the Spring Assembly, the monkeys' complaint, the dead petrel on the island, the old chief and his ice palace, and the voyage to the flag on the bottom of the sea with Pinky Pepper and Flingo. 'I've seen a lot and I met lots of animals,' he beamed.

'Dolphins and hamsters are nice animals and vultures are actually quite okay too.'

Snail didn't understand it all, but listened carefully anyway, because Mr Finney was his best friend.

'Speaking of arguments,' Snail said after a while. 'Can't this Flingo of yours help solve our argument with the squirrel?'

That was the last thing Mr Finney wanted to think about right then. It was far too pleasant sitting there drinking tea with Snail. But Snail persisted.

'Have you seen the mountain of beechnut shells the squirrel has tossed into the garden?'

'Ah, we don't need Flingo for that.'

Snail looked surprised. It was the first time Mr Finney had stayed so calm about the squirrel. 'Why not? Don't you think the shells are important anymore?'

'Of course, I do,' Mr Finney answered, almost laughing at Snail's indignant expression. 'But I've learnt a thing or two on my travels!' He jumped up and walked out into the garden. 'Squirrel!' he called. 'You there?'

It stayed quiet.

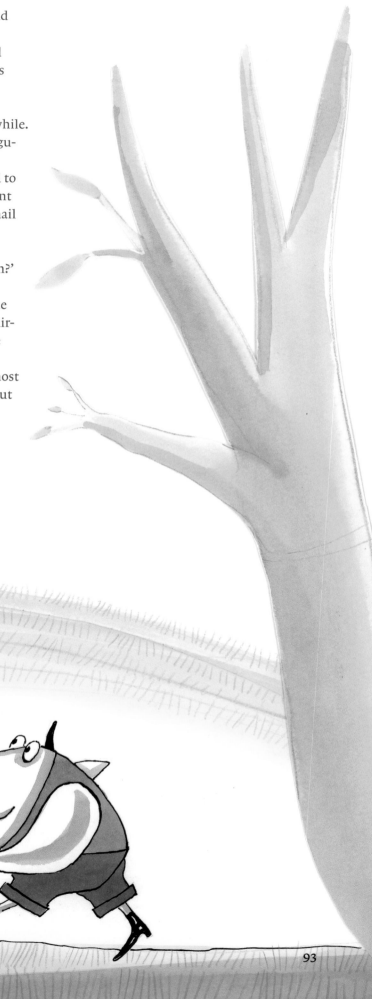

'Squirrel, it's me, Mr Finney!' he called a few times. 'I'd like to talk to you!'

'Yeah, yeah,' they heard Squirrel say. 'I know who you are! I suppose you want to complain about our beechnut shells again? It was so nice and peaceful while you were away.'

Mr Finney laughed. 'You won't believe it,' he said, 'but I don't want to talk about your rubbish at all.'

Now the squirrel came out from behind a bush.

'I wanted to give you this bit of the garden,' Mr Finney said. 'Then it will be yours and you can throw as many beechnut shells there as you like!'

'Why the change of heart?' the squirrel asked suspiciously.

'Ah,' said Mr Finney, 'otherwise I'll just keep on asking you to stop. And this land belonged to everyone once.'

'But, Mr Finney, that's the nicest thing I've ever heard,' the squirrel said. 'You know what, from now on I'll shell my nuts somewhere else. Just keep your garden.' The squirrel ran to the edge of the garden and disappeared up a tree.

Mr Finney walked back to his house happily. But suddenly he gasped. He had completely forgotten that he still had a task to carry out! Pulling the old chief's seeds out of his pocket, he decided to ask Snail for advice.

'These are seeds from trees,' Mr Finney began.

'Are we going to plant them?' asked Snail.

'I'd like to,' replied Mr Finney. 'But I promised I'd take them to the right place. I'm just not exactly sure where that is.'

'But surely your garden is the best place in the whole world?' Snail was surprised that Mr Finney hadn't thought of that himself.

Mr Finney shook his head. 'Not for these seeds,' he said. 'We have to look after them until there aren't any more trees. And the seeds will only keep somewhere cold.'

'Like ice cream?' Snail asked. 'Then we can just put them in the freezer?'

Mr Finney thought about it. 'You're right,' he said after a while. Relieved that Snail had helped him, he gave him one of the seeds. 'I'll put the bag in the freezer, but we'll plant this seed together in the garden,' he said, sure that the old chief would approve.

'Thank you,' said Snail, slightly dazed. 'This is probably the most beautiful present I've ever had. This seed will grow into a big tree and then I'll have my own favourite tree!'

Mr Finney nodded. 'And that tree will bear new seeds,' he said, 'that even more big trees will be able to grow out of!' He had only just closed his mouth when he realised that he, all by himself, had thought of a solution for the problems of the monkeys and the other forest animals. For every tree that was cut down, Snail and he would simply plant a new tree! 'Then the monkeys won't need to worry anymore,' he told Snail. 'The old chief was right: solutions are sometimes closer than you think.'

Snail looked at him questioningly.

'I'll explain later,' Mr Finney said with a yawn, 'but if you don't mind, I'll go have a nap first. I've been flying all night.'

'Goodnight, Mr Finney,' said Snail. 'I'm glad you're home.'

When Mr Finney was finally in bed, he thought for a moment about Pinky Pepper. It had been fun to go travelling with her, he knew that now, but coming home to Snail was fun too.

Outside, it had started to rain. Listening to the drops on the roof above his head, Mr Finney felt his eyelids slowly getting heavy. He fell into a deep sleep.